Harmless

ALSO BY DANA REINHARDT

A Brief Chapter in My Impossible Life

How to Build a House

Harmless

DANA REINHARDT

WENDY LAMB BOOKS

Published by Wendy Lamb Books
an imprint of Random House Children's Books
a division of Random House, Inc.
New York

This is a work of fiction. Names, characters, places, and incidents either are the product of the author's imagination or are used fictitiously. Any resemblance to actual persons, living or dead, events, or locales is entirely coincidental.

Copyright © 2007 by Dana Reinhardt

All rights reserved.

Wendy Lamb Books and colophon are registered trademarks of Random House, Inc.

Visit us on the Web! www.randomhouse.com/teens

Educators and librarians, for a variety of teaching tools, visit us at www.randomhouse.com/teachers

The Library of Congress has cataloged the hardcover edition of this work as follows:
Reinhardt, Dana.
Harmless / Dana Reinhardt.
p. cm.
Summary: When Anna, Emma, and Mariah concoct a story about why they are late getting home one Friday night, their lie has unimaginable consequences for the girls, their families, and the community.
ISBN: 978-0-385-74699-1 (trade) — ISBN: 978-0-385-90941-9 (lib. bdg.)
[1. Honesty—Fiction. 2. Conduct of life—Fiction. 3. Interpersonal relations—Fiction.] I. Title.
PZ7.R2753 Har 2007
[Fic]—dc22
2006029359

ISBN: 978-0-553-49497-6 (trade pbk.)

Printed in the United States of America
10 9 8 7 6
First Trade Paperback Edition

Random House Children's Books supports the First Amendment and celebrates the right to read.

For Daniel

Anna

This is what I know about the truth: the farther you get away from it, or it gets away from you, the harder it is to tell.

If only I had told the truth that night.

Life would have gone on. Life has gone on, but everything is different. I wish more than anything that I could go back to that night, walk in my front door, and undo everything we did.

This is the story of what really happened. This is the truth.

I knew Mariah was hanging out with a guy from the local high school. Everyone knew. That's what it's like when you go to a school as small as ours. I wasn't one of the girls Mariah would peel down her turtleneck and show her hickeys to, but I'd heard about them. I'd heard they were the size of golf balls and as dark as overripe plums. I wished she would show them to me. I wished she would pull me into the bathroom and block the door with her black Converse high-top and say "Check this out" and I'd gasp and then we'd both be late to our next class. But Mariah never gave me the time of day.

It was Emma who first brought me into Mariah's orbit. They were assigned a scene from *Romeo and Juliet*. They had to rehearse it and then perform it for their English class. Emma was playing Romeo because there's a shortage of boys in our school. Maybe that's why Mariah was hanging out with the guy from the public high school, although really, I think she was just trying to be different. To stand out. To be talked about. And probably to get away from all the boys in gray slacks and navy V-neck sweaters we're trapped with day after day after day.

I don't think anybody really knew what "hanging out" meant, but most of us chose to believe it meant "having sex," and that gave Mariah even more of an edge than she already had. It's hard to stand out in a school where everyone wears the same uniform and everyone lives in the same community and everyone's parents work either at the college or for CompuCorp. But Mariah managed to stand out. She was pretty, but not girly. Smart, but not a teacher's pet. Boys liked her. Girls wanted to be like her. There is no other way to say it: she was the coolest person in school, or at the very least, she was the coolest person in the freshman class.

So when Emma was assigned to be her Romeo she couldn't

stop talking about Mariah this and Mariah that. Finally she invited me to her house one afternoon when Mariah was coming over to work on their scene.

Emma's been my best friend since third grade, when she moved here from the city. Her parents are literature professors at the college. They live only two blocks away and her older brother, Silas, was a senior who somehow managed not to look dorky in our school uniform. He wanted to go to Columbia next year and even though I knew Columbia was only an hour and fifteen minutes away by train, I still secretly hoped he wouldn't get in.

When I got to Emma's house, they were down in the basement, drinking lemonade and eating Oreos. They'd both changed into jeans and Mariah was wearing a tank top and right away I could see the hickeys. They looked like they ached, like if I reached my hand over and touched one, she'd wince.

I sat down in a beanbag chair and threw my backpack on the floor. My plaid skirt felt itchier than usual. Why didn't I think to change my clothes?

"Hey, Anna Banana," Mariah said, and she dipped her Oreo into her lemonade.

Anna Banana. It's what my dad used to call me when I was a little kid and no matter how hard I try I can't get him to break the habit. But for some reason, coming from Mariah, I kind of liked the way it sounded.

"What're you doing here?" she asked.

I looked over at Emma, but she just sat there, twirling her finger in her hair and staring at her lines. "I'm always over here," I said. The beanbag chair was disappearing beneath me. I readjusted the stuffing. "I practically live over here."

"That's cool. Wanna be our audience?"

"Sure," I said.

She smiled at me. "Feel free to applaud wildly when we're done."

They stood up and I stayed in the beanbag. Emma was pretty good, but she seemed a little uncomfortable and stiff, and Mariah was amazing and beautiful. I could see why a guy like Romeo might kill himself over her.

After that we just sat around and talked and I got to hear firsthand about DJ and his car and his favorite leather jacket that he gave her and even about the hickeys. She said he had some really cool friends and we should all hang out sometime and I probably should have just said "No thanks" but I didn't because she's Mariah and I'm just plain old ordinary Anna with nothing at all to show for it.

Emma

I wish we'd never left the city. My parents always talked about how much better it would be for everyone if we could have a real house with a real yard in a real neighborhood where we could ride our bikes up and down the tree-lined streets. Well, New York City is real too, real in a different way, and I don't know why everyone seems to think life in the country is so much better. And safer. It's not. I know that for a fact.

New York City gets a bad reputation up here. Take Central Park. People always talk about it like it's some scary place where you should never go alone, but for me growing up, that's where I fed my first duck and where I hit a triple in T-ball. Or take the place down the block from our apartment where Silas and I would get ice cream cones. The guy who worked there used to give us free sprinkles. Does that sound dangerous to you? Does that sound scary?

Sometimes Silas calls me *Emmalus Painintheassicus*. That's my species name. It's a joke we have because there's this zoo in London where they have people in cages, and he threatened to send in my name for one of the few coveted spots. Thousands of people applied. Thousands! This boggles my mind. Why would you want all those strange eyes watching your every move?

The only explanation I can come up with is that none of these people live in a small town like I do, because if any of them did, they'd already know what it feels like to live in a cage.

It's not like I hate it here. In fact, I used to like it here just fine. But now there's a part of me that wishes I were back in the city, taking a subway or a bus to school instead of walking. I wish there were so many people in my grade that I couldn't know everyone's name even if I wanted to. If I went to school in New York and something happened to me, not everyone would know about it because New York has so much else going on, who would ever care about what happened to me, or about what I did?

It doesn't seem fair to blame Mariah, but any way you look at it, that's where this all started.

Mariah and Anna and I started hanging out because of that stupid English class assignment where I had to be Romeo. I didn't want to be Romeo. I've tried hard to shake my tomboy image, including wearing eyeliner and shaving my legs, even though my mom says I'm too young to do those things. She says I shouldn't buy into the male-dominated ideal of feminine beauty, which to me is just professor-speak for it's hard for her to watch me grow up. Anyway, I didn't think playing Romeo would do much for me in the image department. But at least I got paired with Mariah. It could have been worse. Then again, when you look at the big picture, I guess it could have been a lot better.

I could tell Anna was jealous that I was talking to Mariah and that we were sitting together during study hall and that she was coming over to my house after school. Anna's like that. She kind of freaks out whenever she thinks I'm making new friends. But I'd made a resolution at the beginning of freshman year to broaden my social circle and here it was January already, half the year had gone by, and there was nobody until Mariah.

Finally I just told Anna she should come over because I was kind of getting sick of her asking me all these questions about Mariah. What's she like? Have you seen her hickeys? What's up with her boyfriend? Whatever.

She's fine. I haven't seen her hickeys. And I saw DJ once when he picked Mariah up at my house.

He drove an old lime-green station wagon with wood paneling. Not exactly a tough-guy car, and the truth is, he didn't look like much of a tough guy. He was a little pudgy with really big eyes and dark hair and dimples and a tiny diamond earring. I'm sure everyone at school pictured him as some kind of tattooed badass who chain-smoked and strangled live puppies for sport, but that's just because everyone at our school thinks that people who don't live in our neighborhood and wear our stupid uniform every day are scary. Just like they think New York City is scary.

When Mariah talked about DJ, at first it was kind of annoying, like she was bragging and all: look how cool I am, I have a boyfriend and he's older and he drives a car with a roomy backseat . . . if you know what I mean. Anna was really impressed. You could just tell by the way she stared at Mariah, with her mouth slightly open and her eyes big as moons. Not me. Unlike Anna, I'd actually had a boyfriend once, though I didn't anymore.

Silas had a girlfriend. She was a senior like him and her name was Bronwyn and she had curly brown hair and freckles and really long legs. She was pretty cool. Whenever she saw me in the halls or in the cafeteria she came over and talked to me. Once she even took me shopping. Silas and Bronwyn made everything seem so easy. They were good-looking and in love and happy. Maybe they were so happy because they knew they got to go off to college in the fall. Silas said he didn't know what was going to happen with them next year, but I could totally see them staying together and then getting married and having kids and living in an apartment in the city that wasn't too far a walk from Central Park.

Mariah told us that DJ had some cute friends. She wanted to plan a party at his house. He'd bring some people and she'd bring Anna and me. I was supposed to be broadening my social circle, so I said sure. Why not?

Mariah

Carl thinks this whole thing is my fault. It doesn't even matter what really happened—whatever the story, Carl would find a way to blame everything on me. He's an asshole, for sure, but I don't know, maybe this one time he's actually right. Maybe everything is all my fault.

Jessica thinks he's some kind of hero, a prince or a knight on a white horse or Batman or maybe even SpongeBob SquarePants. But that's Jessica's world. She's only six. And Carl is her real father. When he comes home from work and he picks her up and spins her around really fast, she looks down at him with the biggest smile and this expression of complete and total devotion on her chubby face. She's a sweet kid and I don't want to be the one to clue her in on the fact that he's an asshole. I'm pretty sure she'll figure that out on her own when she gets a little older. But maybe not. Maybe she'll always look at him that way.

Mom tells me I should give him a break. That he works hard supporting this family. That we're lucky. Ha.

Mom and Carl never even knew about DJ. They would have freaked if they knew I had a boyfriend. And if they knew I had a boyfriend who was older? Who drove? Who went to the public school? Forget about it.

Thank God for Jessica. She kept them busy enough that they weren't in my business all the time.

DJ was seventeen. I met him down by the river one afternoon after school. He was with this group of guys and they had a boom box and they were playing this music really loud that at the time I had no idea what it was but now I know was Ludacris. I was with a couple of kids I used to hang out with before I started hanging out with Emma and Anna. It was early December but it was this crazy warm day that melted all the snow, and the sky was clear and the air smelled great and you just wanted to go be by the river and be outside and obviously I wasn't the only one who felt that way.

I was wearing my uniform. He came over to me and said, "Hey. Shouldn't you be in the library or home baking cookies or doing volunteer work with the elderly or something?"

Right away I noticed his dimples. And he had these amazing eyes that sparkled like when the sun hits the river.

"My homework's all done and there's a big plate of cookies that's been cooling on the windowsill since just after I finished helping the old lady cross the street." Pretty quick comeback, if I do say so myself. Then I leaned in a little closer to him and added, "I think I've earned a sip of whatever it is in that paper bag you're holding."

My fingers brushed against his when I took the bottle from him. It burned my throat but I tried not to let that show. We started talking and before I knew it his friends had disappeared. The music had stopped. The sky was turning pink just above the hills. My so-called friends who I don't even talk to anymore, probably because I started going out with DJ and that broke some kind of code of conduct or something, asked me if I was ready to go, but I told them to leave without me. DJ asked if I wanted a ride home. Even though I'm only about a ten-minute walk from the river I said sure.

I'm not an irresponsible person. I know the dangers of getting in a car with a boy you don't know. Especially if he's been drinking something that burns your throat and comes concealed in a paper bag. But I wasn't worried about DJ. I felt like I already knew him. And anyway, we left the bottle down by the river and I could tell that he hadn't really had much more than a few sips. He hadn't even brought the bottle. One of his friends had.

The truth is I wanted to make out with him. I wanted to feel his lips on mine and even his hands on my body.

"You're really cute," he said when we were both sitting in his car.

"Yeah, you too."

Then he started kissing me and we barely ever stopped.
Until we stopped.

I knew people talked about me. Some people probably thought I was a slut. Some probably thought I was bitchy. Some people probably thought I was stuck up because I lived in a huge house with a swimming pool. They didn't know how I used to live before Mom met Carl. They didn't know anything about me. Nothing at all.

Anna

Things started to change for me right away when I became friends with Mariah. People started to notice me. Nothing against Emma. She's always been my best friend, but when we were together all the time, just the two of us, we were kind of invisible. Now there was Mariah and Emma and me. MariahEmmaAnna. Three best friends. Three is the magic number.

Getting noticed reminded me of those days just before and after each of my early-childhood birthday parties. I used to have these huge parties. Because my parents didn't want anyone to have hurt feelings, they insisted I invite every single kid in my class. I remember going to school with a big bundle of brightly colored envelopes and I remember all the little hands scrambling for one to tear open. Bowling! Pizza! A puppet show! I remember the excited whispers. And the Monday after, there was still talk about Anna and her party.

But by Tuesday or Wednesday, just as sure as the shredded paper from the brightly colored envelopes of my thank-you cards was swept up and put in the trash, I was forgotten.

I'm an only child. It's just me, Mom and Dad. Three makes a family. But I wanted a sister. I would have even settled for a brother but what I really wanted was a big sister, which, my mom always pointed out, was biologically impossible. When I then asked why I couldn't have a *little* sister she would tell me that I filled them with as much joy as they could ever imagine. She said they wanted me to have every opportunity in life and to have everything I needed and they were worried that they wouldn't be able to give me all that if there were more mouths to feed.

Mom waited until I turned thirteen to tell me that three didn't make a family: they'd really wanted to have another child, and they'd tried and tried and they'd even had two miscarriages before they finally gave up. I guess she figured I was old enough to finally hear the truth. I don't know if all those other stories about the love I filled them with, and wanting me to have opportunities, and worrying about mouths to feed, were lies or half-truths.

I'm not really sure what the difference is anyway.

Sometimes at night when I'm alone in my room and the lights are out and the house is quiet I try to picture them. My two little miscarried siblings. A sister and a brother. I named them Ruby and Silas. I've always loved the name Ruby, and Silas, well, Silas is Silas. He's just the best brother in the whole world. I picture my Ruby and Silas with curly red hair, which is funny because nobody in my family has red hair. Or curls. I guess when I think about it, in my mind they kind of look like the Raggedy Ann and Andy I kept with me in my bed until I was ten and realized the time had come to give them up. I don't know what happened to them. They just disappeared from my life.

Since I'm an only child I tend to get a lot of attention from my parents. My mom has flexible job hours, which means she's home when I get back from school every day. She runs a program at the college for kids who come from poor neighborhoods and underperforming high schools. She helps them fit in. She's not a professor like Emma's parents. She's an administrator, which doesn't come with an impressive title or a big office. I used to feel lucky, but having Mom here all the time started to get on my nerves when I wanted to spend more time hanging out with Mariah. And Emma, of course.

Sometimes we'd go to Emma's house. This wasn't a problem because Mom's used to me going to Emma's after school. At Emma's the three of us would sit in the basement and listen to music and talk and complain about our teachers. Sometimes we'd go down by the river or walk along the train tracks or just sit out in the fields behind school when none of the teams had practice. On those days I'd tell Mom that I was working in the library. She said fine as long as I came home before dark.

I was convinced that Mariah and DJ were doing it even

though she never came out and said so and I never asked. But that's what happens when you date an older guy. I was pretty sure Silas and Bronwyn were doing it. You could just tell by the way they looked at each other like they had the most wonderful secret in the world between them. I hadn't seen Mariah and DJ together but I was sure they looked at each other the very same way.

She talked to him a lot on her cell phone but he wasn't really around that much. He was always just about to show up and then he'd call, or sometimes he wouldn't, because something came up. The few times he did show she would leave us and hop into his car and he would wave from the driver's seat and they'd be off. I'd watch his green station wagon speed down the road with a big hollow feeling in the bottom of my stomach.

They were planning a party at his house when his parents were going to be out of town. It was going to be a small party. Just their closest friends. That meant Emma and me. Me. I was one of Mariah's closest friends.

Emma

When we first moved up here I wouldn't come out of my room for three days. My parents tried bribing me and then threatening me and finally they just brought in dinner on a tray and we all sat on my floor and ate spaghetti carbonara. On the fourth day my mom knocked on the door and told me there was someone here to see me. Anna walked in. She had straight brown hair and bangs. She was about my height but heavier than me and her toes pointed in a little and it looked as if her shoes were two sizes bigger than mine.

"I heard you just moved into the neighborhood and you'll be going to my school."

"Where'd you hear that?"

"My mom. She's downstairs. Do you wanna come over to my house?"

And with that I left my room. I went over to Anna's and then we played every day until school started, by which time I was already known as Anna's best friend, Emma. That was six years ago. Now I'm three inches taller than she is.

Sometimes I wonder if we'd ever have become friends if her mom hadn't made her come over that day. If I'd just started third grade as the new kid from the city who didn't know anybody maybe I would have become best friends with Sharon Bender or Tammy Frost or someone else or nobody. But that isn't how it happened. We became Anna and Emma.

It's not like I never had any other friends. The kids at school have always been pretty nice to me. I've hung out with other people, but whenever it would get to something I'd do more than once or twice, Anna was always there, asking what's up with you and so-and-so or inviting herself along to the movie or over to my house or whatever. It's a small world at Orsonville Day School. Everyone knew from those first days of third grade that I was paired off with Anna. That's just who I was, I was Anna's best friend, and unlike shedding the tomboy thing, I couldn't just shave my legs and wear mascara to change that.

Maybe that sounds harsh. I don't mean to be harsh. Anna has always been a very loyal friend, and that counts for something. It counts for more than that; it counts for a lot. I mean, one thing we know about animals in captivity is that they need companionship. For starters, nobody wants to go to the zoo to see lonely monkeys or seals or lions. That's just plain sad. When you go to the zoo you want to see monkeys picking things out of each other's fur or seals touching noses underwater or lions lazily swatting their tails at the rocky earth, napping side by side.

Mariah was the first person to come along who didn't seem to mind having Anna around and this made me like Mariah even more. The three of us were quickly becoming the best of friends. My social circle was growing.

One afternoon after Anna and Mariah left my house Silas came down to the basement. He was just getting back from basketball practice.

"What's up with that chick Mariah?"

"She's my friend."

"Awwww. How sweet. E.P. has a new friend." E.P. Short for: *Emmalus Painintheassicus*.

"Shut up, Silas." Why was it that I could never come up with a rude species name for him?

"You should know this about your new friend: lots of people talk about her. Lots of guys do. Guys in my class."

"Yeah, what do they say?"

"They think she's hot."

"Well, she has a boyfriend."

"I heard. Some guy from Orsonville High?"

"Yeah. DJ. He's cool." I still hadn't ever talked to DJ but I wanted Silas to think I knew him. I wanted Silas to know I had a life; that my circle was expanding. "He's older. He's a senior."

Silas bounced his basketball a few times on the floor. Then he started bouncing it off the wall. He fixed his eyes on me. "Well, all I can say is be careful."

I now ask myself why I didn't listen to Silas when I have to admit, as strange as it sounds, I don't think he's ever been wrong about anything.

But I didn't listen. Instead I grabbed the basketball from him. "What's that supposed to mean?"

"I don't know. You're still a kid and she seems different. She seems older than you."

"Well, she's not. She's three months younger than me. And anyway, I'm not a kid."

He took his basketball back and cradled it in his lap. He looked carefully at me. Maybe he was reevaluating me. Trying to see me differently. Trying to see through the bars, beyond the description next to my cage. *Emmalus Painintheassicus*: generic human little sister.

"It's just that I can't picture you going out with a senior. That wouldn't be right. That would mean you'd be going out with someone in my class and it's just that I know those guys too well to let any of them go anywhere near you."

So I was wrong about the way he was looking at me, but I didn't hold that against him. I guess it goes both ways. I had a hard time seeing what everyone else saw in Silas. Silas the senior, the star athlete, the Columbia-bound perfect boyfriend with a killer body. I still know things about Silas. I know that certain movies make him cry and that his farts make our dog get up and leave the room. That's the thing about being in a family. No matter how old I get and no matter what happens to me or any of us, I'll always be his little sister and he'll always be my big brother.

At least I hope this is true.

The party at DJ's was on. It was going to be on a Friday

night. Mariah suggested I tell my parents I was sleeping at Anna's. Anna would tell her parents she was sleeping at my house. Mariah would make up something else, she said she'd done it before and it was no problem. She said we'd have nothing to worry about.

Mariah

I didn't start at ODS until seventh grade. ODS stands for Orsonville Day School, but everyone just calls it ODS, which is pretty funny because it sounds like you're saying *Odious*, and if you ask me, that name suits this school perfectly. By the time I got here everyone was already established in little cliques and everyone knew everything about everyone else because that's what happens when you all go to school together from the time you're five years old.

    I spent seventh grade as kind of a loner. I spent most of eighth grade with this group of really annoying girls who never talked to anyone else and finally stopped talking to me when I dared to sit with other people during lunch. That's when I decided to avoid cliques altogether. This year I had a few different friends before I met DJ and before I started spending the time that I wasn't spending with him with Emma and Anna. I knew some people thought they were losers, especially Anna, but I didn't care. At least Emma and Anna were cool enough to want to get out of Odious and maybe meet some of DJ's friends from Orsonville High.

Before we moved here, I lived in Dexter County. It's about forty-five minutes away. I didn't go to a private school because there is no private school in Dexter County and also we didn't have much money then. It was just Mom and me in our little apartment and she worked a lot and sometimes that was hard, but in other ways it was easier than it is now even though we live in a big house with a pool. For one thing, there was no Jessica. Now, even though Mom doesn't work anymore, she has to spend a lot of time on Jessica, taking her to dance classes and piano lessons and even a mother-daughter book club where I guess they don't care if you're really mother and daughter or not.

Mom met Carl online. I think they only went on, like, three dates before he asked her to marry him, and before I knew it we were packing up our apartment and I was writing all these essays about what a great opportunity it would be for me to go to an institution as well regarded and academically challenging as Odious. To tell the truth, Carl wrote the essays for me. Or maybe it was his assistant. Or his secretary. I think he has both. We all pretended like I was doing the work but I wasn't. I could have. I'm not a bad writer. I'm also pretty good at math. When it comes to factors and ratios and properties, I know how to solve those kinds of problems.

I wonder sometimes what Carl's online profile looked like. If he were being honest he would have written something like this:

> *Balding middle-aged widower with bad temper, boatloads of money and a motherless daughter seeks pushover with no spine to live in my huge house and take care of my child even if it means ignoring your own. No ugly chicks need apply.*

No worries there. Mom is totally hot. He must have been blown away when she showed up for their first date because even if she had posted a photo, it couldn't have done justice to how truly beautiful she is. She used to be a model when she was younger and she even got some guest-starring roles on a few TV shows that I've never heard of because they were on before I was born. I think people must look at them funny when they're out together, like what's this Beauty doing with that Beast? But then again Carl has a lot of money and I guess that counts for something.

Being with DJ made everything in my life seem more normal. He's who I'd probably have been with anyway if Mom hadn't double-clicked on Carl's Internet profile one day and forever changed my future. We were a lot alike. So what if he was older? I've always felt and acted older than my age. That's what happens to you when you spend most of your life taking care of yourself. So I couldn't imagine dating any of the boys in my class. They were still little boys. DJ was not a boy, he was a guy, and there's a big difference between a boy and a guy. The seniors at Odious are guys too but there's some kind of unwritten rule that if you're a freshman, you stay away from the senior guys or else face the wrath of the senior girls, who manage to scare the crap out of me, even though I don't scare very easily. Especially that girl Tara. She was, like, the ringleader of the bitchy senior girls and she always looked at me like she'd slit my throat if nobody was watching. Anyway, DJ was much cooler than any of the guys at Odious.

I really wanted Emma or Anna to start dating one of DJ's friends. Then DJ and I could be together more. I didn't get to see him all that much because he spent a lot of time with his friends, and it's not like I didn't understand, but sometimes it bummed me out even though I never told him that.

Honestly, it was hard for me to imagine Anna dating any of DJ's friends. It was hard for me to imagine Anna dating anyone. Emma was different. She had potential. She had long, curly blond hair and I know it's a cliché, but guys do tend to like girls with blond hair. She also had pretty big boobs and I figured that couldn't hurt either. She had that total girl-next-door look, complete with the freckled nose and big, open, honest eyes. You take one good look at Emma and you think: here's someone I can totally trust with my deepest darkest secrets. Maybe this made guys shy away from her. Maybe they thought she was too nice, too trustworthy. That's the only explanation I could come up with for why someone who looked like she did in a pair of jeans didn't have a boyfriend. Or maybe it was simply that she spent all her time with Anna.

When Anna wasn't in her uniform she dressed in baggy

khakis and T-shirts, and her shoulders were sort of hunched forward like she was trying to hide what little she had in the chest department. She always wore running shoes and I don't think I'd ever seen her in lipstick even though she could have really used some. Her hair was mousy brown and cut blunt at her shoulders and she almost always had it in a ponytail. She didn't seem to know how to talk to guys. She didn't really seem to know how to talk to anyone other than Emma and me. I noticed the way she was around Emma's brother, Silas. She probably would never admit it, but I could tell that she was madly in love with him even though he was so far out of her league it was ridiculous.

But sometimes people see something in each other even when no one else does. Look at Mom and Carl. So maybe Anna did stand a chance with one of DJ's friends. You never can tell. I invited both of them and I figured we could just wait and see what happened.

Anna

I'd never lied to my parents before. Sure, there were little things like saying I'd finished my homework so I could watch TV when really I had a chapter left to read. There was the time I broke a pair of my dad's reading glasses and then put them back on his desk to let him think maybe he did it, and he never even mentioned it to me. That's a lie too, isn't it? When you fail to tell the truth even if no one asks you? Oh. And I guess there was also that stuff about being in the library after school when really I was hanging out by the river or somewhere in town with Emma and Mariah, but that didn't feel like such a big deal. I had seventh period free and I used to wait in the library for their classes to get out, so when I said I was in the library after school it wasn't a total lie. It was a partial truth.

I was going to tell my parents that I was spending the night at Emma's when really I was going to sleep over with a bunch of other people at the house of a guy I didn't know and there weren't going to be any adults around. This was going to be my first real lie. This was going to be the kind of lie where if my parents knew the truth I'd be in huge trouble. Gigantic trouble. The kind of trouble I couldn't even imagine, probably because I'd never been in trouble before. But I figured that it took Mom years to tell me she couldn't have another baby. So maybe I'd wait years to tell Mom the truth about where I was going to be on Friday night.

I knew my parents would never check with Emma's parents. Emma's would never check with mine. That's how it was with us. Our parents knew we were always together and they didn't have to call to see if it was okay for one of us to spend the night. Since we lived so close, we always walked to each other's houses, so there would be no dropping us off or picking us up. And also, our parents weren't really friends, so it's not like they would talk and say, "By the way, thanks for letting Anna sleep over the other night." Or "Emma said she had a great time at your house on Friday."

Then again I guess they might say something like that if they were to run into each other in the supermarket or the bank or the dry cleaners, but I was keeping my fingers crossed that that wouldn't happen.

There are those kinds of parents who become best friends just because their kids are best friends. Our parents weren't like that. It's not like they hated each other. They just had very different lives. Emma's parents spent most of their time with other college professors. They were always going to functions at the college that didn't seem to require the presence of my mom, the administrator, or my dad, who works for CompuCorp. Emma's parents had dinners and lectures and cocktail parties and conferences. My parents liked to stay home and hang out with me. We played cards or Pictionary and made our own sundaes and sometimes I'd perform karaoke on the machine we kept in the family room. My parents love to hear me sing. When I was younger I'd put on shows whenever they had friends over to the house. They'd give me standing ovations and Dad would put his fingers in his mouth and make one of those crazy loud whistles that I still can't figure out how to do. I thought I was the best singer in the world. Then I tried out for the musical in seventh grade. Standing on that stage and seeing the look in the eyes of our music teacher and the kids in the audience, I knew right then that those standing ovations at home were just another of those things that parents do for their children. But even now that I know how bad my voice really is, I still perform karaoke for Mom and Dad on those weekend nights when it's just the three of us home alone together.

Mom and Dad always made this big deal all the time about what a perfect kid I was and that made it difficult for me to lie to them. They always told me that I was so smart and mature and that I know how to make the right decisions for myself. They tell me that the best part about being my parents is, no, not listening to my bad karaoke, it's just sitting back and watching me figure out my way through the world. Well, that's what I was doing, wasn't I? Sometimes figuring out your own way through the world means lying to your parents. Sometimes it means taking risks. Making new friends. Meeting new people from different neighborhoods and different backgrounds. Sometimes it means doing things that nobody would ever imagine Anna Banana would do.

I was doing something different. Something new. I was leaving something behind.

I was excited all week long. I had a hard time concentrating in school. My heart was racing. My stomach was in knots, but in a good way. I had a secret. I had a secret that I shared only with Emma and Mariah. We had a three-way secret. Nobody in the plaid skirts or gray pants or navy V-neck sweaters knew that I was going to spend the night at DJ's. But it was true. I was going to spend the night at a senior's house. So maybe he was a senior at Orsonville High, but a senior was a senior as far as I was concerned. The only senior I knew at ODS was Silas. I also knew Bronwyn but I never really liked her all that much. She seemed nice on the surface, but I always felt like that was a façade, like she was only being nice so that everyone would always talk about how nice she was. And perfect. With the ideal boyfriend. She seemed kind of ditzy to me.

After school on Wednesday Mariah and Emma and I met in the library, as usual, but we stayed there this time because it was pouring rain and not showing any signs of letting up. The March sky was black even though it would be several hours before the sun went down. I could go home and tell Mom I'd been in the library, and this time, it would be the God's honest truth.

We had a plan to work out.

"So on Friday you guys should pack your bags and bring them to school and then DJ will pick us up down by the river at five o'clock."

"What should we pack?" I asked.

Mariah laughed. I thought maybe she was laughing at me. But I couldn't help it. This was the first time I'd ever done something like this.

"You know. Stuff that makes it look like you're going to Emma's for the night. It doesn't really matter because I'm sure you won't need anything. Just a change of clothes for the morning. We'll probably stay up hanging out and partying."

Partying?

I guessed this meant drinking. I was hoping it didn't mean anything more than that. See: there's that perfect kid my parents are always talking about. The one who knows how to make all the right decisions for herself. That kid, the one who was finding her own way through the world, knew she didn't want to be at a party where people were doing any drugs.

Our sixth-grade science teacher once told our class about a kid who took LSD and it lasted for a week. His parents found him in the closet, wrapped tightly in bedsheets. He started screaming when they tried to unwrap him. Bloodcurdling screams. He thought he was an orange and he didn't want to be peeled.

That story scared me off drugs for life, not that I ever would have been the kind of person who would have taken drugs in the first place. I've always been cautious, maybe even too cautious.

There was a silence. Emma was acting as if this were all no big deal, like she had spent lots of nights over at some strange guy's house and lied to her parents about it.

"Relax," said Emma with a slight sound of something in her voice. Like she was impatient with me, or just cooler than me. "It's going to be fine."

"I'm relaxed," I snapped back.

Mariah smiled that Juliet smile of hers. "It's going to be more than fine. It's going to be totally fun. I'm so glad you guys are going to get to know DJ. And that he finally gets to meet my two best friends."

She put one hand on each of our knees. Two hands. Two knees. Three friends.

Emma

Silas asked me what I was doing on Friday night. I couldn't figure out where this was coming from. Did he know something? Did anything ever get by him? Maybe his species name should be *Silas Seesallicus*.

I just sat there with a blank face.

"Control room to E.P.: do you compute? Question rendered. Awaiting response."

This was another of Silas's jokes. There's this child robot scientists have been working on in Japan. It has a vocabulary of over ten thousand words and is able to do light housework. Silas says I'm a prototype, that he ordered me over the Internet, and my duties include keeping his room neat, serving his meals and generally obeying his every command.

"Huh?"

"This Friday, you know, the day that immediately follows Thursday. What are you up to?"

"Nothing. Just going to Anna's."

"Oh."

"What?" I said, meaning: what's with the look?

"Nothing. I just thought maybe you'd want to come to the basketball game on Friday night. Bronwyn said she'd give you a ride."

"Much as I'd love to be your little cheerleader and sit in the special section roped off for Fans of Silas, I actually have a life."

"Whatever, kid. Just asking," he said, and then he pinched the skin on my elbow really hard because he knows that's the one part of the human skin where we don't have any real nerve endings.

It was a perfectly reasonable question. Silas knows that on most Friday nights I have nothing to do. I hang around at home, usually with Anna, sometimes with Silas and Bronwyn. My dad is out a lot and on those nights Mom likes to take me to plays and lectures and stuff like that on campus. When I go with her I pretend I'm in college and the guy who's playing the lead in the play is my boyfriend and I'm about to introduce him to my mother and then we'll all go out to dinner and maybe even have a glass of wine.

The truth is I haven't had a boyfriend since seventh grade. That's two whole years. His name was Michael and he still goes to ODS but this year we don't have any classes together.

Back then he was really skinny with kind of a big nose and a mass of tight black curls. Now he's filled out and gotten taller and his nose isn't so big and he goes out with Isabella Rothenberg.

He called me up out of the blue one day and said he had something to tell me.

"I can't just come out and say it, so you're gonna have to guess," he said.

"Okay. Can you at least give me a hint?"

"Sure. It's a three-word sentence with a subject, a verb and a direct object."

We both had Ms. Lockhart for English and he was the star student. Not that this was such a complicated or brilliant little hint, but it did show how he couldn't stop himself from being the class brainiac.

"Hmmm. I don't know." I was playing dumb. Why else would this boy who I hadn't really talked to before call me at home on a Wednesday afternoon to say he had something to tell me? He liked me! A boy liked me! And he was about to tell me he liked me! I remember sitting there with the phone pressed to my ear, writing our names side by side and then enclosing them in a sad little heart.

"Okay. I'm the subject. You're the direct object and the verb is 'to like.' As in I—like—you. That's what I called to tell you."

I knew it.

He asked me if I wanted to go out with him and I didn't hesitate in saying yes. We were a couple all the way up until the summer. We were part of an elite group, cool enough to be going out, which didn't really mean all that much. We almost never went anywhere together. Then summer came and we didn't see each other for three whole months. When we returned for eighth grade he acted like we'd never made out and he'd never put his hand up my shirt, which he had done on five separate occasions. Not that he was mean; he just treated me like some girl who happened to be in Ms. Lockhart's English class with him back when we were both in the seventh grade.

When eighth grade started and I wasn't a couple with Michael I went back to being Anna's best friend. The privileged world of those who have boyfriends closed its iron doors to me.

When Friday finally rolled around, I was ready. It was time to meet new people who didn't know me, not that everyone at ODS really knew me, they only thought they did.

I'd be lying if I didn't say that I was a little nervous about getting into trouble with Mom and Dad. Things had been pretty easy in our house lately. I hadn't heard Mom and Dad fighting in a really long time and I didn't want to give them any new ammunition. I figured that if I got caught lying and sneaking off to a party, then they might start fighting and blaming each other about whose fault it was that I screwed up, and I didn't want to be responsible for starting another Clash of the Calhouns.

I wondered if Silas had ever been in my situation. I wondered if he ever lied about where he was spending the night. I'm not sure Mom and Dad would get so bent out of shape if Silas spent the night at some strange girl's house with no adult supervision. There's a clear double standard in our house and it's not just because Silas is older. It's because Silas is a boy, and I get the sense that Dad takes pride in knowing, or at least assuming, that Silas has a way with girls. Dad was uncomfortable with me even having a boyfriend in seventh grade because he said I was too young. Mom said he was being sexist and that led to a huge blowout, so I stopped mentioning Michael's name around the house. Silas had at least three girlfriends in seventh grade and I can't even count how many hearts he's broken in all the years since we left the city and moved up here. For some reason, that seems to make Dad proud.

I think it's pretty safe to say that even my feminist, girls-should-live-by-the-same-standards-as-boys mom would be beyond pissed off if she knew I was going to be having a sleepover not in Anna's little house with the green trim two blocks away, but in a house the next town over with several older boys who went to Orsonville High.

I think it's also safe to assume that they would hit the roof just knowing that I lied to them because, as they've said for as long as I can remember: We will always be understanding if you promise to always tell us the truth.

That's a bunch of bullshit.

Parents don't really want to know the truth. They just want to know that everything is perfect and that their children are smart and happy and popular and out of danger so they can concentrate on their own problems.

When I sat down to breakfast Friday morning both Mom and Dad were there because one of the many benefits to being a college professor is that sometimes you don't have any classes to teach on Fridays. Or Tuesdays. What a life.

Silas was already gone. Probably picking up Bronwyn before school. I was glad he wasn't home. I'd had a narrow escape with him the other night when he asked me what I was doing, and I knew if it came up again, he'd probably see right through me, Silas-style.

I had my overnight bag by my side. "You guys remember that I'm staying at Anna's tonight, right?"

"Of course, honey. I hope you have a good time." Mom looked up from the paper and smiled at me.

"We will."

"What are you two going to do?" Dad asked.

What kind of question was that? And what was with all the questions anyway? First Silas, now Dad. Why would he ask me what I was going to do at Anna's? He never asks me what I'm going to do at Anna's.

I wondered for a minute if child robots come equipped with self-activating panic buttons.

"I don't know. Nothing. The usual. Hang out. Watch TV."

"That sounds truly edifying." Now that was the Dad I knew. Spouting big words with just a little hint of sarcasm.

"It will be."

I said goodbye and grabbed my backpack and my overnight bag and went outside, where Anna was standing on the sidewalk, waiting for me, with her overnight bag in her hand. We walked to school together like we've done almost every single day since the beginning of third grade.

Mariah

I told Mom we had an overnight class trip to Sturbridge Village. I guess she didn't remember that we had one last year, when I was in eighth grade. She could probably have told you what the second graders were doing every day of the week and every minute of the day because she was a parent advisor to Jessica's second-grade class. Lucky for me they keep the kindergarten through sixth graders on a totally separate campus, so Mom is clueless about what's happening at the upper school and it somehow didn't strike her as strange that the eighth and ninth graders would take the very same field trip.

She did ask if there was any permission slip she had to sign and I just said no, although I thought it would be kind of funny if Mom had to sign a slip giving me permission to sleep over at DJ's.

To whom it may concern:

> I, Shannon Hofstra Dalrymple, grant permission for my daughter, Mariah Hofstra, to spend the night at the home of her boyfriend, who is seventeen years old, turning eighteen in the summer. There will be no adults present to provide supervision, giving them the opportunity to spend the entire night together and wake up in the morning in the same bed.

I'd been waiting for a night like this. The first few times we were together we did it in his bedroom but it was always rushed and he always had to hurry me out before his mom got home. Since then it had mostly been in the backseat of his car. It's not all that comfortable or nice and it's not the kind of place where you want to spend much time after it's over holding each other. You pretty much just want to sit up and stretch your legs out and get your clothes back on.

But tonight was going to be different. I could lie in his arms all night long.

DJ was my first but he doesn't even know it. I managed to grind my teeth through what was a pretty unpleasant experience without shedding a tear or letting out any cries of pain. There wasn't all that much blood afterwards, but what there was he noticed, and I had to tell him I was just getting over my period, which somehow seemed less embarrassing than admitting it was my first time having sex.

I know that people at school assume I've had sex even though I've never bragged about it. I think you can tell with people. Like even though I've never asked her, obviously Anna hasn't had sex. Probably not Emma either.

I told Mom I'd be back by midday on Saturday. She slipped me a twenty and told me to bring Jessica a souvenir. I figured I had a day and a half to come up with a good excuse for why I forgot to bring her back anything and what happened to the twenty.

Carl wasn't a problem because Carl doesn't get involved in where I am or what I'm doing, unless it's to criticize me in some way, like about my room or what I wear or why my grades aren't good enough. He was gone early Friday morning like he is every day of the week. Off to his boring job running some big boring department at boring CompuCorp, where they pay him enough money to have a pool in his backyard.

I met Emma and Anna after school in the library like I always did and we had some time to kill, so we walked into town and I got a cup of coffee and Emma got a tea and Anna got a hot chocolate at the Big Cup, which is our lame town's version of a hip café, and we ran into Silas and Bronwyn. Emma went white as a ghost and that's saying a lot because the girl is seriously fair-skinned. I didn't have time to give Emma a lecture about playing it cool, so I just walked us all over to Silas's table and said hi to them, and Bronwyn gave Emma a big hug. We sat down for a few minutes and then they got up to leave and Silas messed up Emma's hair and said, "Don't get too wild tonight." And he did the same to Anna's hair and then gave my shoulder a squeeze and it was clear that he wasn't suspicious at all.

DJ was half an hour late picking us up but that was okay because it was kind of nice sitting down by the river. It was gray and cool. A big barge worked its way slowly upstream against the current. Nobody else was around, although we did see that homeless guy who hangs out by the river sometimes. He didn't come anywhere near us. Once when I was down there with DJ, the guy looked like he was going to come up to us and maybe ask for money or something and DJ's friend Brian threw a rock at him and now I guess he knows that it's best if he keeps his distance.

We heard a car horn.

"Hello, ladies." DJ rolled down his window. "Hop on in."

We threw our bags in the back and I gave him a long kiss and introduced him to Anna and Emma.

"It's a pleasure," he said, and he smiled one of those smiles that showed off his dimples. "I'm so glad you could make it. Now let's get going and meet the others and get this party started before the keg gets warm."

We climbed into Sally, the name DJ gave to his big green station wagon with the wood paneling, and headed off for his house on Orchard Road.

A bunch of his friends were already there when we arrived. I'd met Brian before but I'd never met Owen or Chris or this girl named Becky who seemed to be the girlfriend of either Owen or Chris. I couldn't tell right away which one. They were all drinking beer out of big red plastic cups and there were four pizza boxes lined up on the dining room table.

Right away, DJ took me up to his room. I didn't even have a chance to meet his friends or make sure Emma and Anna got something to drink, but I figured they could fend for themselves. I brought them there. Now they were on their own.

He closed his door and he started taking off my clothes and kissing me and taking off his clothes and pulling the comforter off his bed. He was moving quickly like on those afternoons when we only had a short window of time before his mom would be getting home. I wanted to slow things down. It had been over two weeks since we'd seen each other. I wanted to talk. I wanted to take our time. I wanted to look at him. I wanted him to look at me. I wanted to tell him something, anything, about Mom or Carl or Jessica. I wanted to tell him how easy it was to lie about where I was going when nobody seemed to care.

But then he whispered in my ear, "I need you."

And I was quiet. There was nothing more for me to say.

Anna

I knew Mariah and DJ were having sex. I just knew it. The minute we arrived at his house they disappeared upstairs. They came back only fifteen minutes later but I could tell that they'd been doing it up there.

You'd think it'd be awkward, just Emma and me and these seniors from Orsonville High while Mariah and DJ were somewhere having sex, but it wasn't awkward at all. We each took a piece of pizza and a beer, which I could barely sip without gagging, and we sat in the living room while that guy Owen, who was really cute, played some stupid PlayStation game against Brian. I sat on the arm of the couch with Owen sitting to my left and watched his hands on the controls. He had a bracelet made of string on one of his wrists.

Emma, I noticed, wasn't having any trouble drinking her beer. She was done and up for another before I'd even finished my slice of pizza. Where did she learn how to drink beer? How did she get so good at it? We'd never been to a party with beer before this one.

I studied Mariah after she rejoined the group. Her face was flushed but instead of having that look in her eyes that Bronwyn does around Silas, she looked a little sad. Maybe it was because DJ didn't spend more time upstairs with her, but this was his house, and he did have to play host, and I figured she should give him a break.

I was relieved when it became clear that the beer was it. There wasn't any talk of drugs or even any liquor, just a suggestion from Owen that we play a drinking game.

It was called Quarters and it involved bouncing a quarter into a cup of beer. I sat down next to Owen, and Emma took the seat on the other side of him. It was a pretty stupid game. Chris and Becky didn't play. Without saying anything, they were gone, and I guessed they were up to the same thing that DJ and Mariah were up to earlier in the evening. So it was just me and Owen and everyone else.

It was getting late. I was getting tired but I didn't want to let that show, so every time I felt a yawn coming on I faked a cough instead. No one picked me to drink the beer with the quarter in it and I was grateful. Maybe all that coughing convinced everyone I was getting sick and they didn't want to get my germs.

I'm sure Emma would have picked me but she wasn't able to get the quarter into the beer. On her best days she's not the most coordinated person I know, but on this night she also happened to be wasted. She'd finished off more beers than I could count. Everyone seemed to be zeroing in on her, choosing her to down the beer, even after it was clear that she was drunk.

She was changing right in front of me. I could see something different in her eyes. She wasn't the Emma I knew. She became this confident person, acting like all these strangers were her best friends, like she was the Queen of Quarters. She was laughing and throwing her head back and twirling her hair in her fingers, but not in her usual absentminded way. Instead she was twirling it in this "hey, look at me and how gorgeous my hair is" kind of way. She took off her sweater and she was wearing a tight T-shirt I'd never seen before. And slowly, she was inching her way closer to Owen. By the time the game was over he had his arm around her, his left arm, the one with the string bracelet, and her hand was on his leg.

I hadn't seen Emma with a guy since Michael Landau in seventh grade and that hardly counted. He was a total dork. I told her what I thought of him lots of times but she didn't seem to care. Going out is way different when you're in seventh grade than it is when you're in high school. In seventh grade you sometimes sit together at lunch or you sit out in the quad during free periods. You don't disappear into someone's bedroom and come back all flushed.

Emma confessed to me, months after she wasn't with Michael anymore, that he had put his hand inside her bra a couple of times on the lawn behind the science center. But still. That was seventh grade. And that had been it. There wasn't anyone between Michael Landau with his hand in her bra and this moment with her hand on Owen's leg.

Emma did have a huge crush on this friend of Silas's everyone called Ax. His real name was Tom Axelrod and he was a senior like Silas and he would hang around the house after basketball practice and tease Emma, and sometimes even grab her in a headlock and make her smell his sweaty armpits, and for some reason this only seemed to make Emma's crush even stronger. But Emma knew nothing would ever come of it. There was an understanding. He was a senior. She just turned fifteen. That doesn't happen at ODS. But here we were, sitting around with a bunch of people we didn't know, and there she was with this guy Owen's arm around her and her hand on his leg like it was the most natural thing in the world. Come to think of it, Owen even looked a little like Ax. He had short spiky hair and dark eyelashes and green eyes and thick muscular arms that you never see on the boys in the freshman class. He was wearing an Orsonville High varsity letter jacket in blue and gold. ODS colors are maroon and gray.

Sitting there with her hand on his leg, with his arm around her, she looked like someone we each someday wanted to be. I just didn't realize it would happen so quickly.

It must have been around two in the morning. Chris and Becky never came back from wherever it was they went. Brian was out on the porch, smoking a cigarette. DJ said he was beat and he took Mariah by the hand and they went upstairs. I'll say this about DJ: he didn't seem to have nearly as much to say to Mariah as he did to his friends, and other than pinching her butt when she would get up to go to the kitchen for more beer or to the bathroom for a pee, he didn't really pay any attention to her. But now that it was time to go to bed, he had a firm grip on her hand.

He told us where the extra blankets and pillows were. It was a small house and the only two bedrooms were occupied. That left a couch in the living room and another in the den.

I went to the linen closet to get pillows and blankets for Emma and me, and when I came back she and Owen were lying next to each other on the couch. Her head was on his chest. She looked like maybe she was already asleep and he was gently stroking her hair. Her hand was still on his leg. I walked over and Owen took a pillow and a blanket from me and said thanks and he covered them up.

"Emma?"

"What?" she mumbled.

"Where are you going to sleep?"

"Right here."

"Should I . . ."

"Just go, Anna."

"But . . ."

"Good night."

Owen smiled at me. "Good night, Anna." He did have a gorgeous smile.

I backed slowly out of the room and retreated to the darkness of the empty den, until I woke up in the middle of the night and came back into the living room, where I saw what I know I saw.

Emma

I woke up in my clothes. I guess I put them back on in the middle of the night, but I couldn't be sure. Everything was a blur, a pounding, achy, uncomfortable blur. I remembered how bold I'd felt the night before and I didn't know where that person had gone. I felt tiny. My circle reduced to an insignificant dot. I was Alice in Wonderland. I'd gone and drunk the Drink Me bottle; now I was lost in a strange and lonely world and I couldn't quite find my way out of it.

I threw up in DJ's parents' bathroom, twice, but that didn't help much. I couldn't purge the night away. I looked in the mirror. Curiouser and curiouser. I decided to take a shower and try to wash away the absent look on my face and the smell of sick. That didn't quite do it, so I put on some of DJ's mom's lotion and a squirt of her perfume.

We all went out to a diner for breakfast. I ordered scrambled eggs but after one bite I knew I'd made a mistake. I pushed them around on my plate and drank my water instead. I sat at one end of the table with Anna and Mariah. DJ and his friends were at the other end, talking and laughing and eating a seemingly endless supply of pancakes. We just sat there quietly, Anna, Mariah and me, as if we were alone, as if we had no interest in what was going on at the other end of the table.

Outside the diner, Owen waved goodbye to me, but he didn't come any closer than the length of a lime-green station wagon.

DJ dropped us off at the same spot by the river where he'd picked us up the night before. He told Mariah he'd call her soon and then he sped off.

We sat down on some rocks.

"So, girls, how'd it go last night?" Mariah asked.

"It was really fun," I lied. It was a pathetic attempt at a lie, but I couldn't seem to muster up any of my newly honed lying skills.

"It was really fun? Come on, Emma. You're not getting off so easily. Tell us everything. What's up with you and Owen? Oh my God, he is so ridiculously hot."

"Nothing really. We made out for a while. I don't really remember. The whole night is kind of a black hole."

Anna was staring at me with her eyes narrowed. "What's that supposed to mean?"

"You know, Anna. A black hole. A void. A vacuum. I drank too much, obviously. Give me a break. My head is about to explode. Do I still smell like beer?"

I leaned into Anna so my shoulder was under her nose.

"No. You smell like some nasty-ass cheap perfume," she said. I'm not quite sure why, but it made me feel good to see her smile just a little bit.

"And that's it?" asked Mariah.

"That's it." It's over. That's all, folks.

Mariah turned her attention to Anna. "What about you and Brian?"

"Gross! God no. He slept on the floor. I was already on the couch. I didn't even know he'd come into the room until he woke me up with his crazy snoring. I had to put two pillows over my head."

I could see Anna was telling the truth. Anna always told the truth.

I was eager to get home. Back to my house. My bedroom. My family. I was tired. And despite my shower, I felt filthy. I took out my cell phone and looked at it. No calls.

We started walking home. Mariah turned off to go toward her house and Anna and I had about another six blocks before we parted ways.

"So are you into him?"

"Owen?"

"Duh."

"I don't know, Anna. Whatever. It was just a fun night." Her smile disappeared. She looked kind of wounded. I felt bad, but on the other hand, she couldn't expect that just because we'd been friends since third grade I had to tell her absolutely everything. I was tired and I needed to be alone.

"I came into the living room, Emma. I saw you."

"Shut up, Anna. You have no idea what you're talking about."

I felt off balance, like I was trying to stand still on a moon bounce while everyone jumped wildly around me. I took in a deep breath. In through the nose. Out through the mouth. I picked a point in the distance to focus on, like they tell you to do when you have motion sickness. A blue door. A blue door to a gray house. A blue door to a gray house, which opens into rooms I don't know, filled with things I've never seen.

My balance returned. I steadied myself, and then I turned and walked away from Anna, heading home, leaving her on the sidewalk looking like the confused little girl she, in so many ways, still was.

My house was empty, but there was a note on the kitchen counter from Mom saying she wanted us all to go to the English department potluck for dinner. The note said: *Silas, honey, why don't you invite Bronwyn?*

I wondered what would happen if I invited Owen.

Was Owen my boyfriend now? Did sharing an itchy floral couch with him mean he was my boyfriend? It was so much simpler in the grammatical days of Michael Landau. I—like—you. Subject, verb, direct object. All right there in the open, nothing left to figure out.

If it was true, if itchy floral couch = boyfriend, then why didn't he say one word to me all morning? Not even goodbye?

Would he call me? Did I care if he called me? How could I not care if he called me after all that had happened between us?

Sleep. What I really needed was sleep.

Mom woke me up when she came home. She was sitting on the edge of my bed and for a minute I thought she knew everything. I thought she knew about the big lie and all the beer and what had happened on the floral couch with Owen, whose last name I didn't even know.

"Hi, honey. Did you guys stay up too late last night?"

"Uh, yeah. I guess we did."

"Well, why don't you get up and take a shower and get ready for the potluck. I made a turkey meat loaf." She gave my butt a smack.

Our shower has never had much pressure and the water doesn't get hot enough. That's what happens when you live in an old creaky house. Our apartment building in the city must have had at least two hundred showers in it and still there was always scalding-hot water and tons of pressure. That's what I needed right then more than anything. Water that could burn my skin with enough pressure to knock me off my feet.

The phone rang as I was getting dressed. Mariah.

"So I talked to DJ and he said that Owen wants to see you again."

"Really?"

"Yeah. I think he's totally into you."

"Are you sure?"

"Yes, Emma, I'm sure. We were talking about maybe all going to DJ's again Friday after school. His mom's going out of town and his dad's on the night shift. He'll be home at midnight, so we can't sleep over. We can just say we're going to a movie or something. What do you think?"

I wasn't sure what to think. I should have been thrilled. Owen wanted to see me. Mariah said he was "totally into" me. Owen liked me. Subject, verb, direct object. But why didn't it seem so simple?

Lying to my parents was proving to be remarkably easy. I thought of that commercial with that guy who screams, "At these prices, you can't afford *not* to shop at Eddie's!" So I guess I figured, when it's this easy to lie, I can't afford not to.

"Sure, I guess."

"Cool. It'll be great. Probably just you and Owen and me and DJ."

"Listen, Mariah. I have to go to this stupid potluck thing at the college with my family. . . ."

"Say no more. I understand."

She hung up.

I sat there for a minute listening to the dial tone—its low, lonely, hollow sound—like a child robot, not knowing how to feel.

Mariah

When I got home, Mom asked me how the field trip was. She was sitting at the table, sorting through a stack of glossy brochures.

"You know Sturbridge Village. It never changes. What's all this stuff?"

She pushed her hair back from her beautiful face and let out an exasperated sigh.

"Oh, Carl thinks we should take a trip this summer and I'm trying to find something appropriate for kids."

"I'm easy. I'll go pretty much anywhere as long as I can sleep late and order room service," I said, but I was thinking about what it would feel like to be away from DJ and I was hoping we were talking about a short trip here.

"I mean something appropriate for little kids. I know you're easy, Pumpkin. You've always been a dream." She reached out and squeezed my hand. She held up one of the brochures. "I'm thinking maybe a Disney cruise. How does that sound?"

"That sounds odious." How I loved that word. "Really, Mom, maybe that would have sounded good, like, seven years ago or something, but do we all have to be stuck out at sea with Mickey and company, twenty-four seven, just to keep little Jessica happy?"

"Mariah."

That was Mom's way of saying "enough." Or a kinder, gentler version of "shut up." And I didn't really blame her for the way she said my name or for giving me that look. I wasn't being fair. I don't hold anything against Jessica. She's only six and she lost her mother and I'm happy for her that she has Mom now. She loves Mom. How could she not? And obviously Mom loves her too or else she wouldn't be contemplating a Disney cruise.

"Whatever, Mom," I said, and started to leave the room.

"Did you remember the souvenir? For Jess?"

Oh. Right. So I told her this story about how someone must have ripped off that twenty because after I'd picked out this mini butter churner, I looked in my wallet and it was empty. She shook her head like "what a shame." I told her not to tell Carl because I was sure he'd go all apoplectic and call his friends on the board and demand some kind of investigation or something and that would be embarrassing for me. Mom nodded like she understood and she stroked my hair, and gave my hand another squeeze, and promised she'd keep quiet.

Funny. I'd lied to my mother, stolen her money, spent the night with my boyfriend, and managed to get her to feel sorry for me. I was a genius.

Everything was falling into place. If it worked out with Owen and Emma then I could see a lot more of DJ. Maybe the four of us could go out to a movie or go to a real restaurant or even take a drive to Albany to see some band perform at the Arena. I wondered if Ludacris ever made it to Albany.

And maybe, just maybe, if Mom and Carl saw that someone like Emma, who gets straight As, whose brother is going to Columbia next year, and whose parents are professors of literature, was going out with Owen from Orsonville High, then they wouldn't mind that I was going out with DJ. His prom was in a few weeks. I was hoping he could come pick me up at my house instead of down by the river.

I still didn't know why Carl would even care who I went out with, but he did. He talked a lot about our image in the community and how everything I did reflected on him. He was always in my business about how I wore too much makeup or my skirt was too short or my attitude was too sassy. That's the word he used: *sassy*. What a dick. I guess he just wanted me to set some kind of virginal example for his little angel-princess Jessica. He wanted me to be the Disney version of the perfect older sister.

It was Saturday night and I had nothing to do. Mom and Carl were taking Jessica to a kids' movie, and not like I felt like spending two hours watching a talking armadillo, but they didn't even ask if I wanted to come along. I called DJ. I thought maybe he could come over for a quick visit and then disappear before they returned, but he just let his voice mail pick up even though I called him three times in a row and sent him two instant messages.

Emma was at a potluck with her parents and Silas. There was no one else I could call, so I called Anna. She invited me over for dinner and even though that sounded like a lame thing to do, eating dinner with Anna and her parents on a Saturday night, I didn't exactly have any other options.

I left the house without a coat and realized halfway through my walk to Anna's that this was a mistake. By the time her dad opened the door my teeth were chattering.

He put his arm around me and said, "Mariah. It's so nice to meet you. We've heard so much about you."

He was short and stocky, with a big warm smile and tufts of hair visible over the neck of his T-shirt. His hug felt sort of cozy. He was the opposite of Carl. He was a teddy bear. Carl's more like a G.I. Joe.

He told me to call him Wally and then he yelled up the stairs for Anna, who came racing down them like the house was on fire.

Her mom came out of the kitchen and wiped her hands on her apron. She was short too, a couple of inches shorter than me, with big boobs, but not the good kind of big boobs. They were the kind of big boobs that looked like a shelf sticking out from her chest: something she could rest her arms on, or maybe a book or a mug of coffee. She had long straight hair that was braided into a rope down her back, too many freckles and big brown eyes. My mom's a former model. Anna's can make a mean lasagna. I ate three helpings.

I wouldn't have ever believed it, but halfway through dinner I found myself envying Anna. She has this perfect little family of just her and her mom and dad and a warm little house and an old wooden dinner table with lots of scratches in it. Ours gets polished probably three times a week and I can see Carl's reflection in it whenever we're eating together. Believe me, one view of Carl is more than anyone should have to stomach, especially while you're eating.

This could have been my life if my mom had married my real father. Just the three of us. Laughing and talking with our mouths full of lasagna. But I guess for her to have married my real father she would have had to know him in the first place, and she didn't. He was some guy at a party. Or maybe a guy she met while she was on a shoot. She wasn't really sure. It never mattered much to me because I had Mom and I had her all to myself.

Then Carl came along.

"So, Mariah, what do your folks do?" asked Anna's mom, whose name I learned was Carolyn.

"My mom mostly takes care of my little stepsister, Jessica. And she, you know, takes yoga and she volunteers and stuff like that."

"And your father?"

"You mean my stepfather? I have no idea. Something at CompuCorp."

"He's vice president in charge of sales and new-product development," said Wally. Then he saw my confused expression and added, "Carl Dalrymple. I work under him."

"Poor you."

Wally laughed. He didn't say anything about me being wrong.

Then, before I even knew what I was saying, I added, "My real father lives in Los Angeles. He's an actor."

"Really? That's exciting. What have we seen him in?" asked Carolyn.

"He mostly does theater. Serious stuff. He's really talented. He's won a bunch of awards." It was amazing how easy it was for me to picture this made-up father of mine. There he was, standing alone on a stage, a light shining down on him, his hands clutching a statue, and his eyes motionless, locked on mine.

Later, up in Anna's room, she started pressing me about Owen and Emma.

"So did Emma tell you anything more about what really happened with Owen?"

"What do you mean?"

"I mean, they slept in the same room. Do you really buy that all they did was make out?"

Wait a minute. Weren't Anna and Emma supposed to be best friends? Hadn't they known each other forever? Weren't they close like sisters? Why was she asking me all this? Why didn't she just talk to Emma?

"I don't know. But I do know that he likes her. He wants to see her again."

"Really? When? Where?"

Even though I was pretty good at lying, I couldn't come up with anything on the spot. "This Friday at DJ's. We're going to say that we're going to the movies."

"That sounds easy enough."

Anna's room looked like it must have looked back when she was a kid, like she'd been in this house forever and had never had to move to some strange new place. There was an old, frayed stuffed dog on her bed missing one of its droopy eyes. She still had picture books on her bookshelves. Her walls were pink and white stripes.

I could see how much she wanted to go with us and at that moment, I didn't have the heart to disappoint her.

Anna

I know what I saw. I may be inexperienced. I may never have kissed a boy or had his hand in my shirt, but I know what I saw. I just didn't get why Emma was lying to me. I kind of thought it was Emma's duty as my best friend to tell me more, but for some reason she was acting like this was too private to talk about and I just couldn't understand that. Emma and I talk about everything. At least we used to. I gave her every opportunity to tell me the truth. We walked back to her house, just the two of us, but she still didn't say anything.

I stood on the sidewalk after she turned onto her street and watched her keep walking away from me until she got smaller and smaller and finally disappeared up her driveway and I was left all alone.

Mariah had no problem telling me things. She came over for dinner and it was totally embarrassing because Mom and Dad were giving her the third degree, asking her all kinds of questions, but at least they never suggested we take out the karaoke machine. Then Mariah and I hung out in my room, just the two of us, and that was cool because we'd never hung out just the two of us without Emma around. She told me about how she and DJ had been having sex since about the second week they knew each other. She said it made their relationship really strong. I guess maybe he's different around her when they're alone, just the two of them, up in his room.

Two. Two is the magic number.

At school the next week I kind of thought Emma would walk around like Mariah used to with everyone whispering about how she was dating this senior from Orsonville High, but that didn't happen. Emma kept it to herself, and nobody seemed to pick up on anything, probably because nobody could imagine Emma doing something as daring as spending the night on a couch with a guy she didn't know. Emma was just Emma. She wasn't Mariah. And everyone knew it.

I tried to get more out of her about her night with Owen, but she shut me out. Suddenly, after all our years as best friends, she wasn't sharing the details, which was kind of annoying because I'd heard details about everything else in her life. I could draw a perfect map of her apartment in New York City even though someone else has lived there for the past six years. I know the names of all thirteen of her cousins. I can sing the entire song from the camp she went to for four summers, and I never even visited her there.

I know some more private things about her too. Serious things. I know about how her dad was accused of sexual harassment by a student when he used to teach in the city and that's one of the reasons they moved up here. I know this about her because she told me one night. She'd overheard her parents fighting about it and she was crying, and she whispered the whole story to me in the dark while I was lying in a sleeping bag on the floor of her room. We haven't talked about it since. I tried once to bring it up but she acted like she had no idea what I was talking about.

That was what she was doing now. Acting like she had no idea what I was talking about when I'd ask her what happened that night with Owen.

So I stopped asking.

For the first time in my life, I wasn't Anna Banana, the perfect kid who makes all the right decisions. I was becoming Anna, with her own life and her own friends, who goes off to do her own things.

We were going back to DJ's and I was hoping there'd be someone better for me to hang out with than Brian. He wasn't that cute and his snoring almost peeled the wallpaper off the walls. Mariah decided we would tell our parents we were seeing some movie adapted from a Jane Austen book. She chose it because it was playing at the college campus theater and that's the only theater we can walk to. Also, it's long and that meant we could come home a little past eleven without any questions asked.

I was a pro at this now. I figured last Friday was the Big Lie, and this was just the little lie and we could pull this one off, no problem at all.

Emma

On Friday night Silas and Bronwyn rented two Will Ferrell movies and I wanted to stay home with them and sit on the couch and eat ice cream and get into my pajamas and laugh at Will Ferrell and his stupid sense of humor. Now, more than anything in the world, I wish I had done just that.

I can't really explain why I went back, other than that I thought I was supposed to want to go back. There are rules, I guess. Laws of science. Let's call this one the Senior Boy–Freshman Girl Principle. When a boy like Owen likes you and wants to see you again, you go. You have no choice.

But I knew the minute I saw him that the last thing I wanted was to be alone somewhere with him, so I spent the entire night avoiding him. And this time, I also stayed away from the beer.

Lots of stuff happened that night. It was the night of surprises. For one thing, Anna spent most of the night out on the back porch, making out with Brian. Who could have predicted that? And Mariah and DJ got in a huge fight. I had no idea Mariah could scream like that. She's always so cool and laid-back, but we could all hear her screaming even though she was upstairs, behind his closed bedroom door, and we were all downstairs with loud music playing on the stereo.

But what's really important about that night at DJ's is that my cell phone rang at 10:45. It was Mom. I was smart enough not to answer, and when I checked the message she sounded hysterical.

She and Dad had a dinner on campus that let out early and they decided to come to the Jane Austen movie. She searched the theater for me, but the lights had already gone down. Now it was over and I wasn't there and where was I and she'd already called Anna's mom and even got a number for Mariah's house and talked to her mom and no one had heard from any of us and WHERE ARE YOU?????

Species name: *Motherus Hystericalus*.

I ran upstairs and pounded on DJ's door even though Mariah was still screaming at him.

I quickly told her that we were busted and she grabbed her purse and said, "Come on, asshole. We need a ride home."

"Screw you," said DJ. "You can walk."

We ran downstairs and found Anna, who was still all over Brian, and even though he's kind of gross and seems like a big dumb jock, he, unlike DJ, was cool enough to at least give us a ride. This time, it was me who left without saying goodbye to Owen.

Brian dropped us down by the river.

This was bad. We couldn't get caught. If our parents found out we were at DJ's this night then they'd figure out we'd been at DJ's the Friday before, and there are certain things that parents must never know.

Anna just sat there with her head in her hands mumbling, "Ohmygodohmygodohmygod."

Poor Anna. Her body was tense with worry. She pulled into herself hard, like one of the rocks we were sitting on.

What would happen when her parents realized she wasn't the perfect, always-on-her-best-behavior only child they thought she was?

Screaming Mariah had turned back into Cool Collected Mariah. She was acting like this whole mess was no big deal.

"He is such a prick. I give him, like, everything. I'm always there for him. I really thought he loved me even though he never said it. I could just tell. And now he says he's bringing some skank from his class to his prom? I thought he was going to ask me tonight. I really did. I've been slowly stashing away money from Carl's wallet to pay for a dress and everything."

I didn't really see what this had to do with our current circumstance. Prom dresses? Really.

"Mariah," I said. "This is huge. We're busted. Everyone knows we weren't at the movies. What are we going to do? We can't tell them about going to DJ's. We can't do that."

Mariah walked over to the edge of the river, picked up a

stone and threw it as far as she could. It disappeared. It didn't make a sound when it hit the water, like the night just swallowed it up.

"I was a virgin," she said, just like that.

We were quiet. I felt the sting of those words, sharp behind my eyes, aching in my body, my heart. I sat down. I looked at my watch. I could barely see the numbers. My head was underwater. I squinted my eyes and managed to focus. 11:00.

"I'm sorry." That was all I could think to say.

She sat down again and looked over at Anna.

"Hey, Anna Banana. Chill. Take a breath."

Anna looked up. She unfolded. Even though there was no moon, only the tiny twinkling lights from other people's houses across the river, I could see that her eyes were filling with tears. "But what—"

"Don't worry. Let's put our heads together. We can handle this. We can figure something out. We'll come up with something."

Mariah was right. We could figure something out. A story. A lie. We tell lies all the time. Sometimes it's easier to tell lies than it is to tell the truth.

It was then, there in the darkness, with only those little pinpoints of light to see by, light from a world away where other people with their own problems and their own secrets lived their own lives, that everything in our world changed for good.

Mariah

DJ stands for Darryl Junior. He always hated being called Darryl, which is what his mother called him. His dad sometimes called him Junior. He hated that even more.

DarrylDarrylDarrylDarryl. JuniorJuniorJuniorJunior.

DJ stands for Dumb Jackass. DJ stands for Dim-witted Jerkoff.

It was all suddenly clear. He didn't care about me. He was just using me. He never planned on taking me to his prom or introducing me to his parents or treating me like a real girlfriend. The minute after we left he probably had a big laugh with all of his stupid, stupid friends about how I went all psycho on him when he told me he was bringing someone from his class, Kat, to the prom instead of me. Kat. She sounded like a stuck-up prissy bitch.

To top it all off we were busted and sitting down by the river in the dark trying to figure out what to tell our parents. I was going to be in trouble. Big trouble. I was going to get in big trouble over that Dumb Jackass. That Dim-witted Jerkoff.

Emma's mom called my mom and there was a message on my voice mail and Mom was trying to sound calm, but I could hear Carl yelling in the background. I wasn't going to get away with this and I was a liar and he'd had enough of me and my attitude and yell, scream, yell, scream, yell.

Anna was totally freaking out and I just kind of wished I'd never taken pity on her in her little girly room the other night and invited her to come. She was making it hard for me to think.

We didn't have much time. It was getting late. Now it was later than we said we'd be home, which didn't really matter because everyone already knew that we hadn't been to the movie anyway. We couldn't say that we'd been at DJ's. Emma was right. That was out of the question. Mom and Carl couldn't find out about DJ. Not that way. I couldn't even imagine what would happen if they knew I'd spent the night with him. Yes I could. Carl would talk about sending me to boarding school again but this time it might be more than an empty threat.

"We could say we changed our minds about the movie and went out to eat instead."

Stupid Anna. That would never work. She was so simple-minded sometimes. Where did we go and why didn't we call and why weren't we home already?

"We could say we went to a different movie."

"How did we get there, Anna? Who drove us there? Who drove us home? How is that going to work?"

"Jeez, Mariah. At least I'm trying to come up with something here."

Emma was sitting there without saying a word. At least she wasn't whining like Anna. Then she sat up and looked at me with those honest eyes of hers.

"We could say something happened to us, something bad...."

Something bad *had* happened. DJ told me he was taking stuck-up prissy Kat to his prom. He told me this *after* having sex with me.

Emma went on: "We could say something bad happened. Something bad happened to me."

Emma was starting to make some sense.

Here's our story:

It was a nice evening. We had some time to kill, so we came down to the river to watch the sun go down. We were sitting around talking, watching the boats, listening to the crickets, and we lost track of time. When we realized that we weren't going to make the movie we decided to go to the Big Cup and have some hot chocolate and then go home early. But there wasn't any hurry since we could get hot chocolate anytime, so we kept talking. We were alone. It was getting dark. There was no moon, but the stars were beautiful. We lay down on our backs to see if we could find the constellations Mr. Krause had been teaching us about in science class.

We don't know what direction he came from. He seemed to just appear out of nowhere. He grabbed Emma. We all started screaming but there was nobody around to hear us. He told us to shut up. He said if we kept on screaming like that he'd kill us. He said he had a knife.

He took our cell phones. He didn't want us calling 911.

He told Mariah and Anna to stay down on the ground. If we moved an inch, he said, he wasn't afraid of using that knife.

He picked Emma up and dragged her a few feet away. He told her to take off her clothes. Emma said no. He said take off your clothes *now*.

Mariah felt around on the ground next to her. She grabbed hold of a rock slightly bigger than her fist. She showed it to Anna in the darkness. They quietly shifted onto their knees, keeping low to the ground. His back was to them and Emma was sobbing. She was starting to unbutton her shirt.

Mariah jumped up and lunged at him with the rock in her hand. She struck him in the head. He doubled over. Anna kicked him hard in the back. Then we ran.

We ran through the woods lining the river. We ran as fast as we could. We came to a landing by the water with a dock people use to launch their motorboats. We crouched underneath it. We waited. We wanted to make sure he hadn't followed us. We wanted to make sure it was safe to walk home. Our hearts were pounding. We didn't make a sound. We don't know how long we stayed there under the dock. It could have been ten minutes. It could have been three hours. We didn't know. We couldn't be sure.

Anna

I guess it goes without saying that Mom and Dad were up and waiting for me when I got home. Every light in the house was on, and as I approached it from the sidewalk it looked warm and welcoming in the darkness.

I heard Mom shout, "She's here!" as I took the first step up to the front door.

Dad threw his arms around me. "Oh, thank God!" He kissed the top of my head. Then he took a quick step back. There we were, just my parents and me, home together like we would have been on any normal Friday night. But on this night, they were looking at me in a way they'd never looked at me before. They folded their arms across their chests. They wanted an explanation.

Mom touched my cheek with her hand. "You've been crying."

I have the kind of face that gets all red and splotchy when I cry. There's no hiding it. Even if I'd had the opportunity to splash cold water on my face, which I hadn't, or had the chance to borrow some makeup from Mariah, which I hadn't, Mom would still have been able to tell that I'd been crying. And for some reason, when she pointed this out, I started crying all over again.

They led me over to the couch and sat on either side of me.

"Why don't you tell us what happened? Where have you been? What's going on?"

I tried, but the words wouldn't come. Dad rubbed my back. The phone rang. None of us made a move to answer it. Then we heard Emma's mom's voice on the machine.

"Carolyn? Wally? Are you there? It's Pamela. We need to talk about this. Emma is very shaken up, understandably. How's Anna doing? Let's get together in the morning. I think we need to go to the police. I'll call Shannon, Mariah's mother. For now let's just hold our daughters close. Sleep well. All of you."

Click. Dial tone. Silence. Mom and Dad's eyes on me.

I took a deep breath and I started to tell them the story. The first few words were almost impossible, but then, as I went on, I was surprised at how easy it was. How naturally the details came to me. How clearly I could picture the whole incident.

". . . And then Mariah grabbed a rock and showed it to me and without saying a word I knew what we had to do. . . ."

It was just like putting on a show, without a karaoke machine, and with my heart beating hard in my chest.

". . . We ran and ran through the woods by the river until we came to a dock. . . ."

When I finished there was no standing ovation. No loud whistles. This was a new kind of performance for me.

Dad started pacing the room. This is what Dad does. He's a pacer. Mom took the blue cotton throw blanket and wrapped it around my shoulders even though I wasn't cold in the slightest.

Mom and Dad believed it all. There was no question about that.

"We have to do something about this," Dad was saying. "We can't allow this to happen."

"It did happen, Wally. It happened to our little girl."

"Dad. Mom. I'm fine now. Really. I mean it. Let's just forget about this." This was supposed to be it. The end. Tell the story and you will be forgiven.

"How can we forget about this?" Mom was the one crying now. Her hands were shaking. I felt something spreading through me. Heat. Sickness. Nausea.

"Everything's okay. Can't we just pretend this didn't happen?" Please? Pretty please? Trust me, pretending is easy.

I'd told the story to my parents and they believed it and I wasn't in trouble for lying or going to DJ's or making out with Brian or anything. Now it should all be over and done with and I swear, I promise, I won't lie about where I'm going ever again if we can just STOP TALKING ABOUT THIS.

Dad grabbed a spiral notebook and one of my pens and pulled up a chair so he was facing me.

"Tell me every detail you can remember, Anna. I know you've had a long night but I'm afraid things will get fuzzier in the morning and it's important that we make a note of everything you can remember so we can give it to the police."

"The police?" I knew this would happen. I just knew it. I asked, right there by the river, "What about the police?" Mariah said it wouldn't be a problem. She said our parents wouldn't make us go if we didn't want to, they wouldn't want everyone knowing, and anyway, even if we had to go to the police, she said, we had nothing to worry about because the police are idiots. Nothing to worry about. That's what Mariah always said. And I always listened to her.

"Of course. We have to go to the police."

"No we don't. I told you. I'm fine. Look at me."

"You're lucky, Anna, and also very, very brave. But we can't let anyone get away with this. What if this happens again, to someone who isn't as lucky or as brave as you?"

"It won't happen again."

"You don't know that."

"Yes I do. Dad, please. I don't want to go to the police."

"I'm sorry, Anna Banana. This is just something you have to do."

It's hard for me to remember what else I said that night. What exactly I told my father. I remember only that he was taking notes with my purple felt-tip pen and our story looked absurd written out like that in purple ink. I kept to the script and when his questions called for specifics I was as vague as possible. He was medium-size. I don't remember what he was wearing. I don't know what he looked like. I can't be sure. I don't remember. I don't know. It was dark. I was scared. I wasn't thinking clearly.

Sometime during all this my mother was able to calm down and stop crying and turn her attention to me, which meant supplying me with things to keep me warm: more blankets, some hot tea. Did I want her to draw me a bath?

She was just trying to help. It wasn't her fault. She couldn't have known that the last thing I needed was heat.

She couldn't have seen the white-hot shame that was burning deep inside me.

Emma

By lunchtime on Monday everyone knew. But that was Monday. On Sunday Silas and I took a train into New York City, just the two of us, and got ice cream and took a walk in the park and then rode home with the river on our left as the sun was setting and just sat there side by side. On Saturday we went to the police.

I'd never been in a police station. What I learned right away is that they aren't like what you see on TV. They're windowless and dirty with horrible fluorescent lighting and a smell like too many meals reheated in an ancient microwave. Also, they're surprisingly quiet. I don't know what I expected to see. Maybe lots of people in handcuffs and people running in screaming, "Help! Officer, I need help!" or at least telephones ringing off the hook. I didn't expect to see a bunch of people in bad-fitting polyester uniforms sitting around looking bored.

The detective who took our statements was named Scott Stevens. He was tall and lanky with ears that stuck out and a goofy smile and kind eyes and everyone around the station called him Scotty but we called him Detective Stevens. Anna and Mariah and I told Detective Stevens everything we knew, which was, basically, nothing.

We kept our answers vague. We didn't know what direction he came from. We didn't know what he looked like. How tall he was. What color eyes. What color hair. If he had any distinguishing features. Detective Stevens pointed out that I was in the best position of the three of us to get a good look, but I told him that I was so frightened it was like I was having one of those experiences people talk about having right before they die, when they float out of themselves and observe the scene from above. I was out of my body, watching from someplace else, seeing only shapes in the darkness.

Detective Stevens was patient. When he listened he had the habit of tugging at his ears as if that might make him hear more than what was being said. He didn't push us. He offered us sodas from the machine in the hall. We told him what we knew and he wrote it all down. When we said we didn't know something, he said that was fine, that we shouldn't worry about it, and he smiled one of his goofy smiles, which were really more sweet than goofy. After a little over an hour he led us out to our parents, who were waiting in the lobby, and they took us all home.

Mom ordered some pizzas and Dad canceled a dinner he had and the four of us sat around the table and tried to pretend like everything was normal. Everything *was* normal. Everything was normal before I became friends with Mariah. Now I couldn't sit and eat a piece of pizza without Mom and Dad and Silas staring at me like I'd grown a second head.

Mom tried talking about a trip to Chicago to visit my grandparents over the summer, but then out of nowhere Dad slammed his fists on the table and shouted, "Goddammit."

"Raymond," Mom said, which really meant: *Raymond, don't do that, calm down, you're overreacting in that annoying way you do.*

This is what it was like with Mom and Dad. There was always a second conversation happening that only they were supposed to understand.

"What? Are you trying to tell me I can't be upset about this? Are you trying to tell me that I can't be furious that some dangerous miscreant, some soulless felon tried to . . . to . . . to attack my only daughter?"

The word he chose not to say hung heavily in the air above us all.

Rape.

It echoed silently in every corner of the room. It seeped into our clothes. Our food. The walls around us. I didn't want to hear it. I didn't want to think about it.

I thought instead about the Arctic Circle. I read about this group of French scientists who were camped out at the Arctic Circle, studying the shape of the earth beneath its surface. Everyone assumes the inside of the earth is shaped just like the outside. I remember the diagrams in my fifth-grade textbook of different-colored concentric circles.

But maybe if you cut the earth in half you wouldn't find

perfectly rounded layers, one tucked neatly inside the next. Maybe my textbook was wrong. Maybe on the inside, the earth's just a big, unruly, indefinable mess.

I envied those scientists and the months they would spend trying to figure this out, surrounded only by the Arctic's white nothingness.

Mom paused and took the sharp edge off her voice. "What I'm trying to tell you, Raymond, is that we need to be here for Emma right now. We need to concentrate on supporting her."

"Well, I think we need to figure out who did this to her and then do something about it."

"That is the typical male response. Fix it. Do something. Men never deal with the emotional truth of the situation. Look at her, Raymond. Look at her."

"Can we please stop talking about me in the third person?"

I put my head down on the table and closed my eyes.

Silas pushed his chair back and stood up. "Hey, Em. Let's leave these freaks and go watch some bad TV."

He put his arm around me and led me downstairs. Mom and Dad stayed at the table and we could hear their whispering voices from the depths of the basement. It wasn't the kind of whispering full of concern or conspiracy. These were whispered daggers.

Silas reached for the remote control but he didn't turn on the TV. Instead he turned and looked at me. *Silas Seesallicus*.

"Do you want to talk about this?" he asked.

"No."

"All right, then. Let's not. Let's talk about something else."

"Excellent. Great. Perfect."

"Okay. Here are your choices: We can talk about Dalton's law of gas pressure, which, no, does not have to do with my personal gases, it has to do with what's on my AP test next Wednesday. Or we can talk about the bonehead trade Steinbrenner just made, which guarantees that the Yankees stand no chance in this year's pennant race. If neither of those topics does it for you, we can talk about why Bronwyn is so pissed off at me right now."

Silas knows I always want to talk about Bronwyn, to hear more about their relationship and what it's like to love someone and have that someone love you back.

I managed a smile. "I'll take door number three. Bronwyn troubles."

He picked up my feet and put them in his lap and we talked about how he thought they should start school in the fall with a clean slate, without longing for each other, without ties to who they were before they got to college. And even though this wasn't what I wanted to hear, even though I liked to picture Silas and Bronwyn married with a family, forever the perfect couple, it still felt good to me to sit there like that with my brother. He was treating me like a friend, not like a little sister, and for a brief moment, I felt like there wasn't anything in the world that I couldn't tell him.

Mariah

Carl said if I didn't dress like I do and I didn't go hanging around by the river, where people do God knows what, and if I spent more time studying and trying to be a role model for my younger sister, then this never would have happened.

Mom said she was proud of me for being so brave and standing up for myself and my friends and for having the presence of mind to grab a rock, but really, she added, Carl was right, I shouldn't be hanging out down by the river.

Carl got up and left the room.

"Carl's just upset," Mom said. "It's hard for him to deal with difficult things sometimes. You know, he's so protective of you girls."

"Yeah, Mom. Sure."

"No, Pumpkin, I mean it. I know he isn't saying the right things, but trust me, I know him. I know how he sounded, but that's not really what he means. He just wants everything to be perfect. He cares about you."

Then it was my turn to get up and leave the room.

And that's my summary of what happened at Casa Dalrymple in the aftermath of Friday night. The next morning we went to the police.

I tried saying I didn't want to go. I did all the things I told Anna and Emma to do. I begged. *Please don't make me do this. Please. I don't want to talk about this.* But when Carl gets something in his big bald head, sometimes there's just nothing you can do about it. He insisted. And in our house, he makes the rules.

So we went the next day and talked to Detective Stewart or Stevens or whatever his name was. He didn't have a clue. I was pretty sure that was the last we'd ever hear from him. It was time to move on.

DJ was out of my life. I would never, ever talk to him again. My cell phone was lying somewhere at the bottom of the Hudson River, so even if he wanted to reach me, he couldn't. He didn't have my home phone number and he wouldn't have any luck dialing information because I doubted he knew that even though my last name is Hofstra, I live among Dalrymples. I doubted he knew my last name at all.

It didn't matter. I was so over him. I didn't care if he was trying to call me. I imagined my phone vibrating deep under the water, entangled in some weeds, fish giving it a sideways glance as they swam by. Go ahead, DJ. Call all you want. Nobody's around to hear you except for the sad little fish that manage to survive the polluted waters of the Hudson River.

At school on Monday I was sitting in the courtyard before third period when Tammy Frost came over to me. Tammy Frost hadn't talked to me since eighth grade, back when I used to be part of her little group, before I dared to sit somewhere else during lunch. I did overhear her calling me a slut a few months ago, but that's talking about me, which is different than talking to me.

"Oh my God, Mariah. I heard about what happened. Are you totally freaking out or what?" For a minute I thought maybe she heard that DJ had sex with me and then told me he was taking someone else to his prom, but then I realized she was talking about the Incident Down by the River. "I mean, that totally could have been me. I was hanging out there, like, three days before it happened. I never could have done what you guys did. I probably would have just sat there crying quietly and then who knows what that crazy pervert would have done to me."

She was wearing silver eye shadow and way too much mascara, which made it look like she had black boogers on her eyelashes. That may sound gross or mean or both, but that's exactly what it looked like to me.

"I have a free period now, if you feel like talking."

I held up my social studies textbook I'd been trying to skim before class started. I hadn't done the reading. Then again, if word had traveled as quickly as I expected it had, Mr. Langdon probably wouldn't hold the fact that I hadn't done the reading against me.

"Sorry. Social studies calls."

"Do you have Langdon? He's such a dork. Anyway, wanna have lunch together?"

Lunch. With her? I don't think so. This was a road I'd been down before.

"Maybe," I said, because that was what my mom always used to say to me when I was younger, when it was still just the two of us, when she didn't want to start a scene by saying no. I stood up and shoved the book in my bag. "I've gotta run."

I left Tammy Frost, my new best friend (again), who suddenly didn't think I was too much of a slut to have lunch with, and ran to the main building, where my class was about to start. Just as I was rounding the corner, Silas was there.

"Hey, Mariah, do you have a minute?"

"Sure." Silas never talked to me unless I was with Emma. But today it seemed like everyone had something to say to me.

"You don't have a free period, do you? I was thinking we could go somewhere and talk."

What was all this about talking?

"Uh-huh." That was all I was managing to say. "Uh-huh." Here I was with Silas Calhoun, probably the hottest guy at Odious, standing face to face, with nobody else around, and all I could say was "Uh-huh."

"I don't want to keep you from something. You look like you're in a hurry...."

"No. I'm not in a hurry at all. I was just going to my locker." I figured if Langdon didn't care that I hadn't done the reading he'd probably let it slide if I ditched class too. I could stop by his office later and apologize and tell him I was too upset. I'm so sorry, Mr. Langdon, but I really didn't want to be a disruption to the rest of the class, I didn't want to get in the way of anyone else's learning.

We left the building and walked over to this grassy slope that leads down to the athletic fields. It was warm out and the sky was a perfect blue. I took off my sweater. All I was wearing underneath was a tank top. I sat down and leaned back in the grass and let the sun warm my skin. It felt so much better to be here than in Langdon's crappy class.

"I'm worried about Emma. Do you think she's okay? She doesn't seem to want to talk about what happened."

He was wearing a gray ODS T-shirt and when he put his arms behind him and stretched, his shirt pulled tight against his chest and I could see up close why everyone always talks about what a hot body he has. DJ was a lardass compared to Silas.

"She's fine. We're all fine. Sure it was scary, but we all made it out okay. No harm, no foul. Isn't that what they say in the world of basketball?" I sat up next to him.

"I don't know, Mariah. It sounds pretty traumatic to me. But you're probably tougher than Em. I just want to know if there's anything you think I can do to help her."

"Give her some space. Don't press her on it. She probably doesn't want to be bombarded with questions right now. I'm sure she'll be back to herself before you know it."

"I don't know."

"Well, I do. She's going to be fine."

"You think so?"

"I'm certain of it."

He smiled. I was telling him just what he wanted to hear.

"Thanks, Mariah." He stood up and brushed the grass off his pants. He looked down at me and offered his hand. I took it and he pulled me to my feet. "You know . . ." He shook his head. "Sometimes it's hard to believe that you're only a freshman."

Now he was telling me just what I wanted to hear.

Anna

Tammy Frost asked me if I wanted to have lunch with her. Rachel Engel saved a seat for me in Spanish class. Tobey Endo said "Hey" to me as I passed him in the hallway. Tobey never says anything to me. But on the Monday after, Tobey said "Hey" and he smiled a really nice smile at me. Instead of turning red and looking down at my feet, I said "Hey" right back to him.

After we went to see Detective Stevens and told him our story my parents had pretty much given it a rest. I spent Sunday just hanging out in my room and listening to music and while I was lying there I thought about how I, Anna Banana, made out with a guy and he wasn't even some total loser like I thought. He was kind of nice. We kissed for a really long time. It was just like how I always imagined it would be to kiss someone. Warm and wet and dizzy with time standing still. Then Emma and Mariah came running out onto the porch and said we were busted and we had to go home. How had it gotten so late?

I wondered if people knew. If they could see when they looked at me that I was now someone who a boy wanted to spend his whole night kissing. And not just any boy, but a senior named Brian. He even whispered in my ear at one point that I was a really good kisser.

I was sitting in English class thinking about what it would feel like to kiss Tobey Endo. I was sure he'd kissed girls before, but now I'd kissed a boy, so we were even. Ms. Christofar was talking about *The Scarlet Letter*. Usually I do a lot of talking in class, but I'd fallen behind a few chapters. I didn't crack the book all weekend.

All that time, when everyone around me was talking about boys and boyfriends, I was totally missing out.

Suddenly I realized Ms. Christofar had called on me.

"What? I'm sorry. What was the question?"

"Anna. I asked you . . ." She stopped and looked at me and sort of shrugged. "Oh, don't worry about it."

She knew. I could see it in her eyes. Ms. Christofar and Tammy Frost and Rachel Engel and Tobey Endo. They all knew.

"I'm sorry, Ms. Christofar. I'm having a little trouble concentrating today."

"Well, that is perfectly understandable. Would you like to go sit in the nurse's office?"

I looked around. Everyone was staring at me, but not with the oh-poor-Anna-I'm-so-worried-about-her kind of look Ms. Christofar had. They were looking at me like this past weekend I'd just had the best puppet-show birthday party ever.

"No. I'm okay. Really. It's just . . ."

Part of me wanted to crawl under my desk and hide, but there was another part of me that didn't want this moment to end. I wanted it to last for days.

"What is it, Anna?" she said. She walked over to my desk and put a hand on my shoulder.

"Nothing."

"Can I say something?" I turned around. It was Melissa Sands. She was the first girl in our class to get her ears pierced, when we were in second grade. I wanted to get my ears pierced so badly then, but my parents wouldn't let me. I wanted to wear tiny red sparkly stones shaped like hearts.

"Please, Melissa, go ahead," said Ms. Christofar.

"Yeah. I mean, I think it's, like, so cool that Anna and Emma and Mariah stood up to that guy. They did it by themselves and they didn't need to be rescued and that's, like, totally powerful. I don't know how many other girls in this school or anywhere would have been strong enough to do what they did."

"Thank you, Melissa." Ms. Christofar walked quickly back to the front of the classroom to where her copy of *The Scarlet Letter* lay open on her desk.

Hilary Johansson's hand was up. Ms. Christofar nodded at her.

"Hilary?"

"Yeah. I just want to say that I hope the cops find that guy and that he gets the death penalty."

Jonathan, who sits two seats behind me, spoke up without raising his hand. "You can't execute somebody for doing what he did. You can only execute someone for killing somebody else. I'm not defending him. I hope they find him too and that he goes to jail. I'm just saying that the punishment has to fit the crime, that's all. And also I think what Anna and Emma and Mariah did was awesome."

Okay. This was starting to get weird. I'm used to sitting in English class analyzing characters and what happens to them and their actions and motivations. We do this all the time. We just spent thirty minutes doing this with Hester Prynne. That's what English class is for. That and learning about useless things like dangling participles. But there we were talking about me like I was the heroine of some novel or play or short story. Me.

I wasn't used to anyone talking about me at all.

At lunchtime I found Emma sitting all alone. I told her that I, which I figured meant we, had an official invitation to sit at Tammy's table, but she didn't want to go. I looked over to where Tammy and her friends were sitting. I caught Tammy's eye and shrugged and she gave a little wave and then shrugged back and I put down my tray and slid into the seat across from Emma. It felt like the right thing to do, keeping her company. She seemed really down. When I asked what was wrong she just looked at me like I was crazy. I know I was totally freaking out on Friday night and I was sitting there crying, all worried about what would happen, but today Tobey Endo said "Hey" to me in the hallway. Things were looking up.

It's not like I couldn't imagine how she felt. I felt bad at first too about all of this. Really bad. I felt even worse when we all had to go to the police station and talk with Detective Stevens. But now it was over and it was time to put this all behind us. We had a clean slate. We could start over. And even though I wasn't planning on doing anything like that again, it kind of felt like it was worth it. I'd kissed a senior and now we were spending half of English class talking about me instead of some boring book.

What I didn't get was why Emma wasn't talking to me.

"Are your parents giving you a hard time about this?"

"No."

"Are they making you talk about it?"

"No."

"Is this about Owen?"

"God, no. Will you give that a rest?"

She had an untouched plate of chicken fingers and French fries in front of her.

"So what's bothering you?"

"Jesus, Anna. I'm just having a hard time with everything. Can't you understand that?"

"Sure," I said, although I didn't really mean it. I didn't understand anything about Emma anymore. I thought I knew her, I thought I knew everything about her. I thought we had no secrets between us.

But here's something I know about friendship: Sometimes

the right thing to do is to not point out that your friend hasn't touched her chicken fingers or French fries and not point out that maybe she's overreacting. Instead, you just smile and sit with her and say "I understand" when really, you don't understand her at all.

Emma

On Tuesday morning, about halfway through algebra class, this boy named Stuart came into the room and handed a note to Mr. Santiago. He looked up and said, "Emma, Principal Glasser would like to see you in his office."

I'd never been in Glasser's office. Silas and his friends called him Glasser the Harasser, not in a pervy kind of way, even though that's how I thought it made him sound. They called him Glasser the Harasser because he's one of those principals who seem to have no life of their own, so he's always on top of absolutely everything that's happening all the time, no matter how small. He chewed out the varsity basketball team for not being neater in the locker room. He scheduled a meeting with this eleventh grader because he'd become aware that she was throwing away her plastic water bottles rather than placing them in the recycling bin.

But everyone knows that the thing that makes Glasser the maddest is when students skip class, so you know when you get called to his office in the middle of one of your classes, it has to be for something pretty big.

I should have been in a panic. I should have been dizzy and short of breath. Palms sweating. Mind racing. But instead I felt nothing but a dull ache, an endless expanse of white nothingness, filling up the whole of me.

When I got there I saw Anna and Mariah sitting silently on the leather sofa. Their hands were folded in their laps and they were looking down at the floor. I hadn't talked much to either of them since the police station on Saturday, except for lunchtime the day before, when Anna sat down and asked me what was wrong and I just wished she'd go away, and finally she did and she went over and sat at the table with the popular crowd.

Glasser came in and sat behind his desk. He had a beard that I was pretty sure he grew only to mask the fact that he's younger than at least half the teachers at ODS. His desk was covered with pictures of a golden retriever and a small black mutt. No humans in sight.

"Girls," he said, "or, I suppose, the proper way for me to address you is as young women—so, young women, I want to start by saying how proud I am, how proud the entire ODS community is, of you. You have displayed remarkable strength, courage and poise in what I can only imagine is a time of great turmoil. You stand as a shining example to all of us here at Orsonville Day School."

He stood up and walked over to a wall where a large bronze plaque with the school seal on it hung. He used a pen to point to it. "Do you know our motto? *Ad Vitam Paramus?* It is written here, below our seal. *Ad Vitam Paramus:* We are preparing for life."

He considered it for a moment. He tilted his head as if the words might change if he looked at them from a different angle.

"That is what we aim to do at ODS; it is our humble goal. We strive for nothing greater than to send you off into the world prepared for life. Prepared for what this world is and will be and to make certain that you have in your arsenals whatever it takes to meet this world head-on."

I could feel Anna looking at me, but I didn't turn to meet her gaze.

"Here you sit. The three of you. You are only freshmen, and yet you have already proven that we are doing our job. You exemplify our motto. You faced a real-life challenge and you were prepared." He sat on his desk and folded his arms in front of him.

"I want the other members of our community to be thinking about what they might do, given the current climate and the unexpected dangers that lurk outside these walls, to keep safe and avoid this kind of situation. I would like, with your permission, to schedule a special assembly tomorrow morning on community safety." He scratched his beard and then put up his hands, palms facing toward us. "Now, I understand if this idea makes you uncomfortable—if you feel, perhaps, that it draws too much unwanted attention. You each have my permission to skip the assembly and spend the hour in the library doing your homework instead."

There was a pause in the room. A moment of quiet. Glasser walked around to the back of his desk and took his seat again. I was relieved. His energy was making me antsy.

"I think we should be there," said Anna. "This involves us. People already know anyway. What good does it do to hide out in the library?"

Was this Anna talking? Anna who stumbled, big-footed, into my room a few weeks before the start of third grade? Anna was always hiding out. That's what Anna did. She was the expert at hiding out. Once, when we were in sixth grade, our whole class sang "Oh, What a Beautiful Mornin' " before an assembly and Anna retreated to the back, behind the tall girls in the last row, so nobody could see her. Anna thought we should be at an assembly with the entire school where, even if they were guarded and politically correct about it, they would be talking about us? That wasn't the Anna I knew.

"I guess Anna's right. We might as well go," Mariah added.

"Well, okay, then. As long as you're comfortable."

I wasn't comfortable in any way with anything happening in my life but I nodded when Glasser looked at me because I didn't know what else to do right at that moment.

"Let me ask you one more thing," he said. "I know there is all manner of speculation about what happened circulating in these halls as we sit here right now. I wonder whether there isn't an appropriate way to clear things up and set the record straight, without revealing any of the details that might be too personal."

He paused, briefly, as if we were supposed to offer an idea, before he continued.

"I'm thinking of the *Sentinel*. Our award-winning student publication. I hate to pile anything extra on any of you right now, but if you were, again, comfortable with the idea, I think it'd be fantastic if you might write a small article? Your story is inspirational. I think your fellow students will be truly in awe of your strength of character. And I know that they have much to learn from you."

"Sure," said Anna.

"No problem," said Mariah.

They looked eager. Excited by the idea. Anna in particular.

"Why don't you go ahead without me," I said.

When Glasser the Harasser raised his eyebrows I added, "Three people are too many people to write an article. It'll get too confusing."

This seemed to make some sense to him. Three people telling one story. That was hard.

And anyway, what did anyone have to learn from me?

Mariah

When we left Principal Glasser's office we still had about twenty minutes of class time left but no one was there to escort us back to our rooms like they usually did in this Odious prison, so I suggested we go hang out in the quad. Even though it was a beautiful day, the quad was practically empty except for a couple of juniors playing Hacky Sack in their bare feet under a big leafy tree. We sat down in the warm April sun.

"Little Anna is growing up fast," I said. "One minute she's all blubbering about *oh my God what are we going to do boo hoo hoo*, and the next she's offering to write an article about what happened for the ODS *Sentinel*." I couldn't help teasing her; she was such an easy target. Usually she turns red and hangs her head like a wounded puppy but instead she just looked at me and told me to shut up.

"Everyone's talking about us anyway," she said. "We might as well set the record straight."

"How do we do that?"

"You know what I mean, Mariah. We just tell our version of the story and then maybe instead of talking about us, people will start talking to us. In fact," she added, "Tobey Endo talked to me today."

"I thought you were all in love with Brian." I gave her a playful shove.

"Whatever about Brian. He's fine, but Tobey Endo is cute, don't you think? And he goes to school here. With me. Every day."

We both looked over at Emma. She was lying back with her eyes closed and the sun on her face without saying a word. I could see why Silas was worried about her. She was withdrawn and sulky and I felt like telling her to get her act together before she drew too much attention to herself and the whole story. But then I realized she was probably thinking about Owen. She was probably into him and now that I wasn't with DJ anymore she knew she'd never hear from him again. Owen was cute and all but I didn't really get why Emma was taking it so hard. It's not like he had sex with her and then told her he was taking someone else to his prom. She hardly knew Owen.

I felt kind of sorry for her. I patted her knee.

"I'm sorry, Em. I'm sorry this whole thing with the guys from Orsonville High didn't work out. But there are other guys out there. I'm even starting to think I've been wrong all this time about Odious. I think there may be some guys right here in this lame little school of ours."

She still didn't smile. She didn't sit up or open her eyes or give any sign that she even knew there was anyone sitting right beside her.

After school got out I went over to Anna's house to work on the article. Emma caught a ride home with Silas. I saw them getting in his car. He waved at me and I think maybe he even winked at me too.

Anna's mom gave us some brownies she'd baked with peanut butter inside and a glass of milk. I don't think I've had a glass of milk after coming home from school since I was a little kid and lived in Dexter County but I have to admit it tasted damn good. We went upstairs to Anna's room and closed the door.

I sat down on the floor, grabbed a pen and opened up my notebook.

"I was thinking," I said. "We could start with something like: 'You never know what you're capable of until you find yourself staring down the barrel of a gun.'"

That was good. Dramatic. It would get everyone's attention right away. See? I was a pretty good writer.

Anna was standing looking at herself in the full-length mirror attached to the back of her bedroom door.

"It sounds good but that isn't how we said it was. We never said he had a gun. We said he had a knife. And anyway, we said that he said he had a knife. We never even said anything about him pointing the knife at us."

"I was using the barrel of the gun as a metaphor. You know what a metaphor is, right?"

"Of course I do, Mariah. You don't have to patronize me. I'm the one with good grades. I just think talking about a gun is too confusing."

Now she was standing with her back to the mirror, looking over her shoulder. I think she was checking out her butt.

"Right. Okay. How about: 'You never know what you're capable of until you find yourself staring evil in the face'?"

"That's fine. Do you think I need a haircut?"

"A haircut?"

"Yeah. I think I need a haircut. Maybe I should cut it to my shoulders. Or maybe even cut it short like that girl in that movie."

I put the notebook down and stood next to Anna and stared at her reflection.

"Can I be honest with you?"

"Please."

"I think we need to start with your clothes. And maybe some makeup."

"Really? Do you think you could help?" She looked happy, not like the wounded puppy I was so used to. She looked expectant, like a puppy waiting for you to throw back its favorite ball. I took in our two reflections side by side in Anna's mirror.

"Don't worry, Anna," I said. "By the time I'm done with you, you won't even recognize yourself."

Anna

I went to the mall with Mariah. My parents didn't seem to mind that it was a school night. My mom agreed to give us a ride and then return for us two hours later. My dad even slipped me his credit card. I knew lots of girls went shopping with their dads' credit cards but I wasn't one of those girls, or I guess I should say, my dad wasn't one of those dads.

Things had changed.

My mom called Mariah's mom. This was Mariah's idea. She thought her mom would be more likely to say she could go to the mall on a school night if my mom was the one doing the asking. Sure enough, she said fine, and we were on our way with the windows rolled down and my favorite radio station blasting on the stereo even though Mom usually insists on listening to NPR.

First we bought some makeup. We didn't go to one of the counters at the department store like I thought you were supposed to, where the women wear white overcoats as if they practice some kind of medicine. We went instead to Abby's Habit, this little store with dark purple walls and tattooed twenty-somethings looking bored behind the counter, and eye shadow with names like Turquoise Trash and Goblin Green.

The first thing I needed, Mariah said, was to have my eyebrows waxed. I'd never seen this done in the department store, but apparently waxing was one of the specialties at Abby's Habit.

"Why would I want to do that? Won't I look strange without eyebrows?"

Mariah started laughing, but not in a mean way. She put her arm around my neck.

"They don't take your eyebrows off, silly. They just give them some shape."

"I know," I said. "I was joking." This was so obviously not the case, but I think Mariah believed me.

Clementine was the name of the tattooed girl who helped us, and I wondered if this was her real name or just a name she used at work because it sounded like one of Abby's Habit's signature colors. It hurt. Bad. But I didn't wince or cry. I looked in the mirror. I'd never noticed that my eyebrows had lacked shape, but they had. They were too bushy and messy. How could I have walked around all this time with eyebrows like that? Now I looked feminine. Sophisticated. I looked at least a year older and I hadn't even applied any makeup.

My final bill came to almost sixty dollars. I wondered if my dad would freak out. He wasn't much for spending money. Even though everyone in Orsonville knew that the thin-crust pizzas from Giovanni's were far superior, he still insisted we order from Pizza Plaza because they were a few dollars cheaper. I looked in my bag. My sixty bucks had bought me some foundation, powder, blush, two brushes, mascara, four shades of eye shadow and three lipsticks. And the waxing. All in all it seemed like a decent deal. Especially when you compare it to what I spent on clothes at the Pyramid.

We dropped Mariah off and waited in the car until she closed her front door behind her.

"I guess it's good to be the boss," said Mom as she checked out Mariah's huge house from behind the wheel of our Toyota.

Dad didn't even blink about the charges. I offered to pay him back over the summer when I got a job. He gave me a meaningful look and smiled with his eyes in that way only my dad can, and he said, "I hope you enjoyed yourself. You deserve it, kiddo."

I felt a quick jab, somewhere deep in my middle, when I heard Dad say those words: *You deserve it*. The bags felt heavy in my hands as I hauled them upstairs to my room. But when I put on one of my many new skirts and shirts and looked at my eyebrows and the makeup that Clementine had applied for me, I felt much better.

In the morning I tried to make myself look like I did the night before. I tried to remember what Clementine had told me about blending the brown and silver eye shadow but I couldn't pull it off. I wanted to look my best at the assembly, and I soon realized that that required skipping the eye shadow altogether. I used the foundation, the powder, the blush, the mascara and what Mariah called my "daytime" lipstick. I wanted so badly to wear that new skirt and shirt, not my itchy wool ODS jumper and stupid white button-down. I was pretty sure it was against the dress code, but even so I put on this choker I'd bought with black and amber beads. I pulled my hair into a high ponytail.

When I came downstairs for breakfast my mom studied me carefully.

"You look gorgeous, honey."

"Thanks."

"But are you sure it's appropriate to wear makeup like that to school?"

Mom didn't know anything about what was appropriate. If she'd known what was appropriate then maybe it wouldn't have taken me until late in my freshman year of high school to spend time on my appearance. She never wore makeup at all and she never let her hair out of that big nasty braid. Her eyebrows were a mess.

"Yes, Mom," I said. "It's fine. Everyone wears makeup. And anyway, I'm not even wearing any eye shadow."

"If you say so." She sighed and patted the top of my head like I was a child.

Emma met me out on the sidewalk and for the rest of the walk to school she didn't say a word about my new look. I know she noticed. I saw her notice. But for some reason she decided not to comment on the makeup. Or the choker. Or my eyebrows.

"Are you ready for the assembly?" I asked.

"I don't even know what that means. Ready? For what? It's just a stupid community safety assembly. A total waste of time."

I took a deep breath and felt hollow. I missed the old Emma.

I decided to change the subject. "I went to the mall with Mariah last night. I got my eyebrows waxed and a bunch of new makeup and a whole mess of clothes. You should come over today so I can show them to you."

"I can't, Anna," she said, and she looked up at the trees as if she were searching for the source of a sound. I listened. I couldn't hear a thing. She would look anywhere, it seemed, but at me. So we walked in silence. This wasn't unusual. There had been plenty of mornings over the past six years when we didn't speak much on our walk to school. But somehow this felt different.

Maybe she was mad that Mariah and I had gone to the mall without her, that we didn't need her, that we could hang out and have a perfectly good time without having Emma around. Maybe she was still thinking about Owen and what happened or didn't happen on the couch—I couldn't even be sure anymore—and maybe she was wondering if she had a chance with him, if he might still want to be her boyfriend even though DJ and Mariah had broken up.

I was thinking about Tobey. I was wondering if he'd notice my eyebrows.

Finally we arrived at the entrance to the main building just as the bell for first period started ringing in its metallic, blaring, obnoxious way. That's how we know when we're late. I hate being late. But this morning, when I heard that eardrum-shattering ring, I felt relief. Relief that something, anything, was finally piercing the silence between us.

Emma

Special assemblies are always scheduled during third period. That meant no algebra for me, which was the only upside I could see to this whole disaster. I wanted this to stop. I wanted it to go away. I wanted it to disappear. I wanted to disappear.

ODS assemblies are usually a little rowdy. Everyone sits on the gym bleachers and there's a semicircle of folding chairs around the microphone, where the headmaster and the deans sit facing the students. You can always count on one of the football players to shout out something inappropriate or at least fake a really loud farting noise just as someone is about to speak. On this morning, however, everyone sat perfectly still and quiet on the bleachers. I sat in the back, with Silas and Bronwyn, hidden among the seniors. Anna sat with Mariah down in the front row.

Principal Glasser was sitting in the center of the semicircle surrounded by the deans and also Ms. Malachy, the school's crisis counselor. Glasser stood at the microphone looking out at us for a long time before he spoke. There were no inappropriate comments shouted from the audience. No fake farting sound. Finally, he launched into one of his typical way-too-long speeches about the dignified history of our esteemed institution.

"And now our confidence has been compromised." And on and on and on. He listed all the precautions the school was taking, how when we are at school it is the school's duty to keep us safe. *In loco parentis*, he said.

Sitting in the back didn't keep anyone from staring at me. In fact, it made the stares more obvious as all the heads turned around, one after the other. I started trying to keep count, categorizing them using grade and gender and popularity as a kind of classification system, but all the numbers and information started buzzing around in my head, making me feel faint.

Suddenly, I saw the story from a new point of view. Anna and Mariah were heroes, two young girls with the presence of mind to grab a rock and strike back, while I was just the whimpering victim who would have met an unimaginably terrible fate were it not for my two brave saviors.

But wait a minute . . . I was the victim. It was me he grabbed. It was me he ordered to remove my clothes. It was me he planned to do something unthinkable to. Right? That was the story. And I was the victim.

Darby O'Shea, the student body president, stood up from her seat next to Anna in the first row of the bleachers and approached the microphone. The sound of her shoes against the hardwood floor echoed off the far wall of the gym. Darby was probably the most popular girl in school, although Bronwyn had been giving her a run for her money ever since she'd been dating Silas. Darby had thick black hair and blue eyes and a deep raspy voice. She'd been accepted early decision to Harvard, where her boyfriend, Clyde Pressman, was a sophomore. Clyde himself was student body president at ODS two years ago.

She unfolded a piece of yellow lined paper. She looked down at it, back at the semicircle of teachers and then at the students gathered on the bleachers. "Fellow Vikings," she said. It struck me then how absurd it was to have a Viking as a mascot. Weren't Vikings rapists and pillagers? Why did we celebrate Vikings? Was it just the funny hats?

Darby continued, "What happened to these young women could have happened, and could still happen, to any of us gathered here. We are all so grateful that Anna and Emma and Mariah emerged from this nightmare unharmed."

So much for a generic assembly about community safety. Silas gave my knee a protective squeeze.

"But now we must ask ourselves," she went on, "what are we going to do about it?"

"String him up by his balls!" someone shouted from the crowd.

It was oddly comforting to me to hear this and the chuckling that followed it. I was relieved to see that the entire social order hadn't been disrupted: that football players could still be counted on to do what we expected of them.

"Seriously," said Darby. "I think we should organize some kind of schoolwide response to this event. I think we owe this to Anna and Emma and Mariah and we owe this to the greater Orsonville community, of which our school is an important part."

Darby had never once addressed me by my name. I don't mean to say that she was a snob or anything, but she'd never looked at me or smiled at me or even said hello. She'd probably known I was Silas's little sister, but she probably hadn't known my name and she certainly hadn't known Anna's. It may have been a different story with Mariah. Most of the senior girls lived in mortal fear that Mariah would poach one of the boys from their class, but Darby was probably above this, given that her boyfriend was some two hundred miles away. Anyway, it sounded strange to hear her use our names like we were all old friends.

"I'd like to invite someone up here to address us about how we might help to capture this man who threatens our safety. Please welcome Detective Scott Stevens."

Now everyone applauded. How had I missed him in the crowd? He was sitting right there in the second row and when he stood up he looked almost like an exclamation point, his black uniform punctuating the sea of gray flannel. He smiled and nodded at Anna and Mariah as he made his way to the microphone. He'd had a haircut since we'd seen him last and this made his ears stick out even more.

"Hi, everyone."

There was a mumble of "Hi" and "Hey" and "What's up?" from the crowd.

"I'm just here to let you know what we know, which

unfortunately is not very much, about who this attacker is and ask that if any of you has any information that you think might help us in our pursuit of this suspect, that you contact me or any of the officers down at the station. Also, I hope that after I let you know what little we know, you'll be extra vigilant both in the way you conduct yourselves and also in gathering information that might lead to his arrest. Most importantly: Keep your eyes open. Stay alert. Stick together."

Detective Stevens didn't think to readjust the microphone, so he was bent over it in a way that made him look awkward, but I could tell that everyone in the room was taking him seriously. I could only see Anna and Mariah from the back, but I could see that Mariah looked stiff and rigid. Her theory about the police just letting this go was looking kind of flimsy.

When he was done giving his very vague description of the perpetrator (average this, average that), Principal Glasser thanked everyone for coming and said we should all hurry off to our fourth-period classes.

I got up to leave. Detective Stevens was waiting for me as I came down from the back of the bleachers. He gave me a little wave and I stuck out my hand for him to shake and he took it in both of his and held it for a minute, and the tenderness of this act made my eyes fill with tears. He leaned over and said quietly, "Don't worry, Emma. I'm on this case and I don't give up easily."

Just as I reached the door of the gym I felt a hand on my shoulder, another gentle touch. This time it was Ms. Malachy. She told me she wanted me to come see her in her office. She said she thought I looked like I needed someone to talk to.

Mariah

Over dinner, a rubbery pot roast prepared by Constance, the woman who cleans our house and as far as I know has no real credentials in the kitchen, Mom asked me to tell her about the assembly.

"It was fine."

"Just fine? Tell me more. What did they talk about?"

"You know. Community safety."

Carl put his fork down, clenched his jaw and looked at me. "Don't be such a brat. Your mother is talking to you. Answer her."

"I did."

"Seriously, Mariah. I've had it with you and your attitude."

I managed to sneak a quick look at Jessica and I crossed my

eyes and stuck out my tongue. She'd recently lost her two front teeth and she covered the gap in her grin with her little freckled hand. Then I turned back to Carl.

"What do you want me to say? Principal Glasser talked about new rules on campus. We have to, like, sign in and sign out and stuff. And he was all *'in loco parentis'* or some Latin thing for how the school is our family when we're there, and families look out for each other, which is a lot more than I can say for certain people at this table."

He smiled the smile of someone overly pleased with himself. "Now, that is an answer. That is what your mother was looking for. See how easy putting together a real sentence can be?" Then his face darkened. The vein in his big bald forehead was pulsating. "Now, if only you were smart enough to quit while you were ahead. I won't be disrespected at my dinner table. You are excused."

I pushed my chair back and tried to think about how I'd gotten to this moment so that I could remember it and do it again. Not have to sit with Carl at dinner? Not have to eat Constance's disgusting pot roast? I'd won. Victory was mine.

I went to my room and picked up the phone. I decided I should call Emma. She didn't sit with us at the assembly. I saw her afterwards and she really looked upset. I was pretty freaked out too when I saw Detective Stevens there, but I felt better after he talked because hearing him address the school reinforced my first impression of him as a goofball who didn't really seem to know what he was doing. Darby O'Shea probably asked him to be there and he knew he couldn't say no even though he had nothing valuable to say about the so-called investigation. I was going to tell Emma not to worry about Detective Scott Simpleton.

Silas answered the phone. He sounded sleepy even though it was only eight-thirty. I could picture him lying on the couch in the basement watching TV or maybe throwing a basketball up in the air and catching it with his big strong hands.

"Emma's not here. She and my mom are having a girls' night out, which I'm pretty sure involves dumplings and hot-and-sour soup."

"Oh. That sounds cool. So what about you? What are you doing?"

"Just chilling. I'm staring at my books and willing them to impart wisdom to me without my having to actually open them and read them."

"Ah. Well, Silas, tonight is your lucky night. You happen to be on the phone with the master of the closed-book method of learning."

"Oh yeah?" I could hear him shifting his position. Maybe he was sitting up. Or maybe now he was lying down. "Tell me, wise master Mariah. How do you do it?"

"By recognizing that learning is about so much more than what is written on those limited pages. I like to learn through life and its experiences."

"Aren't you, like, fourteen? What do you know about life experiences?"

"More than you could probably guess."

"Hmmm . . . Intriguing . . ."

I felt a bolt of something hot and electric rush through me. Stop, I thought. Breathe. Stay calm.

"Please," he said. "Go on."

I talked to Silas for almost an hour and only hung up because my mom was at my door and wouldn't go away even though I was shooing her with dramatic pantomime motions. She wanted to talk to me about my behavior at the dinner table, and also, she'd snuck me up some rice pudding that made me rethink my earlier assessment of Constance's cooking credentials.

She sat on my bed and yawned. "Jess was hard to get to sleep tonight. She's really excited about this birthday party she's been invited to on Saturday. She wouldn't stop talking about it. But I also suspect that she's bothered by what happened between you and Carl."

"Mom. Really. If you are up here to scold me for making Jessica's bedtime routine tougher on you, I don't think I can handle that."

"No, Pumpkin. That's not why I'm here. I just really want you and Carl to get along better."

"I'm not so sure it's all my fault."

"I'm not saying it is. I'm just asking that you make more of an effort."

"Honestly, Mom. He can be kind of a dick."

"Mariah . . ."

"I mean, blaming me for what happened down by the river is pretty unfair, don't you think?"

"He doesn't blame you. He just thinks you shouldn't have been there in the first place."

The strangest thing was happening to me. I was feeling something heavy in my chest and a tickle in the back of my throat and an itching behind my eyes. Even though this was all just a made-up story, I was bothered by Carl's reaction.

Maybe even more so, I was bothered that I was bothered by Carl's reaction. Why did I care what he thought about me or about what had happened? I felt a tear rolling down my cheek and I didn't make a move to wipe it, hoping that Mom wouldn't notice it and would just say good night and get up and leave me alone in my room. But she's my mom and she reached over and caught it just at my cheekbone. She put her arms around me.

"Oh, Pumpkin. I'm so sorry. I know how hard this is on you. You shouldn't have to be facing all this. This isn't right. You shouldn't have these kinds of worries."

It felt good to have her arms around me, it had been a long time since we'd sat like that, but I wasn't quite sure what to make of what she was whispering in my ear. I couldn't figure out which kinds of worries she was talking about.

Anna

Up to this point in my life, I was sure that I'd always be Anna Banana, that I'd never be part of a popular crowd. I'd go to school dances alone or not at all. I'd hear people talking about parties in the bathroom and I'd take my time washing my hands and drying them so I could gather as many details as possible about who was kissing who and who threw up in whose mom's closet, and I'd file all these details away in my sad and lonely little head. But here I was, nearing the end of my freshman year of high school, and already things were looking better for the next three years than I ever could have hoped for in my wildest imagination.

For one thing, I was pretty sure that Tobey Endo and I were flirting. I couldn't be entirely sure because flirting was new to me, but he did say hi and smile every time he saw me. He called me Hendricks, as in "What's up, Hendricks?" and "Hendricks in the house!" and even though I know addressing each other by your last name is usually something guys do among themselves, being called Hendricks felt much better than being called Anna Banana or, even worse, being called nothing at all.

For another thing, I could sit at Tammy Frost's table at lunch if I wanted to. Emma sometimes wasn't even at lunch, and when she was she didn't seem to care much if I sat with her or not, so I started making a habit of sitting at Tammy's table and listening to her and her friends talk about lipstick shades. What had happened by the river was no longer the big news on campus. Our article came out and people talked about it for another day or two, but there were other things to talk about, like lipstick shades. And boys.

I was debating telling Tammy about my crush on Tobey Endo. On the one hand, it felt against the natural order to talk to someone other than Emma about this. On the other hand, Emma seemed to be impatient with me lately and grumpy and also kind of bitchy and I wasn't sure she deserved to hear my confession or even if she'd care at all. And let's not forget that Emma was not exactly doing a great job of revealing her secrets to me these days.

Tammy had clout. She could make things happen. If I told her, and she told more people, and word got around, and everyone talked about it, maybe it would become something real. But each time I opened my mouth to say something to Tammy, I felt the all-too-familiar heat in my face and I felt the old Anna grab ahold of my vocal cords and squeeze them shut.

I decided to tell Mariah. Even if she didn't have pull with Tobey, she knew more about boys than anyone and I figured she could give me some valuable advice.

We went to the Big Cup after school, just the two of us. I had my first-ever cup of coffee, and with a lot of milk and several spoonfuls of sugar, it tasted pretty good and I wondered why it had taken me so long to make the switch over from hot chocolate. We took a table in the corner and the place was practically empty. There were no other uniforms inside the Big Cup.

I decided to jump right in and I told her I had a confession.

She looked a little nervous and that made me feel even more nervous but I took a deep breath and came out and told her.

"I know this may seem crazy, because he's, like, probably way too cool for me, but I have a pretty big crush on Tobey Endo."

She smiled a huge smile at me. "Christ, Anna. You had me all freaked out there for a minute. Inviting me for coffee. Telling me you had to confess something. You had me worried." She folded her arms in front of her. "So? What are we going to do about this?"

"I don't know."

"Well, I do. We're going to get him for you. He'd be lucky to have you as a girlfriend. Get that into your head, because the first thing you have to stop doing is thinking you aren't cool enough for him. That kind of thinking gets you nowhere, my friend." She stopped for a minute and looked out the window. "I know how you feel. I know what it's like to want someone you think may be out of your reach."

"You do?" Someone out of Mariah's reach? No way.

"I mean, I guess I can imagine what that would feel like. Anyway, look at you, Anna. Tobey Endo would be lucky to have you."

I went home that night and, despite my first encounter with coffee, I slept a deep sleep and dreamed of something wonderful. But when my alarm clock went off the next morning and I reached back for what it was that had left me feeling so warm and content, it wasn't there anymore. The harder I tried to remember what it was, the vaguer my memory of my dream became. I got dressed in my uniform. It looked better in the mirror to me than it ever had before and I went downstairs for breakfast, happy to see my mom and dad sitting at the table, waiting for me.

And then I saw the front page of the paper, her eyes gazing out at me, and just as mysteriously as the warmth from my forgotten dream had come over me, I felt it vanish.

Emma

Her name was Elinor Clements. People called her Ellie.

As I carefully trimmed the edges of the article, I didn't take my eyes off hers.

She was only twelve and lived about forty-five minutes north of here on the other side of the river. She had blond hair like mine, except hers was straight and fell just below her ears, and she had big blue eyes and a gap between her two front teeth. In the photograph she was wearing overalls. She was smiling and squinting into the sun. The caption said she was a junior explorer with the county nature society and that she was an excellent swimmer.

She'd gone missing sometime after school. The last time anyone reported seeing her was at her locker after her last class of the day, an earth science class. Her earth science teacher was interviewed for the article and she said that Elinor was a wonderful student and very respectful of her classmates.

Her best friend, Mandy, who chose not to reveal her last name, was supposed to meet Ellie in the library, where they were going to work on their essays for the sixth-grade graduation contest: "What's in Store for Us?" But Ellie never showed.

Her father owned a big-and-tall men's store in the Kapachuck Mall. Her mother worked as a receptionist at a local veterinarian's office. Neither responded to requests for interviews for this article.

The police had no leads but they stressed that it was too early to assume anything. Kids get upset. They run away. They make irresponsible decisions. Even the good kids like Ellie Clements.

I read the article three times, squeezing out every bit of information there was to squeeze, glued it onto a piece of cardboard so it wouldn't get torn and put it away in my desk drawer, at the top of the pile of articles I've saved throughout the years. Over time, I swear her face started to disappear, worn away from all my hours of staring at it.

When I came out of second period I saw Mariah and Silas sitting together on a bench. They saw me too and they waved me over like they were excited to see me, like it was a surprise to find me in the halls of my own school. "Hurry, Emma, over here! We were just talking about you!" But I kept on walking. I had an appointment with Ms. Malachy.

She'd been on my case to come see her since the school

assembly. I ignored the note in my locker and the one that was hand-delivered to me in English class and finally she was waiting for me the other morning as I was going into gym class, and I figured I'd better agree to see her or else she might follow me into the locker room and we'd be having this discussion with me in my bra and underpants.

I didn't really believe in counseling, but there was something about Ms. Malachy, other than my desire not to have to talk to her in my underwear, that made me agree to see her in her office. She had a gentle voice and she always wore a blue bandana in her hair and she smelled like dirt and honey and she was big and soft and in every way the opposite of my mother. Don't get me wrong, I love my mom. I want to be her someday. She's tall and thin and beautiful and glamorous and intellectual and when she tells a story the entire room hangs on her every word. But Ms. Malachy seemed like the kind of woman you could show your messiest self to and not have to worry that you were letting her down in some way.

I liked her office. It was cluttered and small and the couch was an ugly shade of orange with a big tear in one of the cushions. The office had high ceilings and a small octagonal stained-glass window above her desk that gave the room an almost churchlike feel.

"Forgive me, Ms. Malachy, for I have sinned. It has been forever since my last confession."

"You've sinned?"

"I was joking. It just feels like a confessional in here, what with the stained glass and the close quarters, not that I've ever been in a confessional, but I've seen them on TV."

She looked around and smiled. "Yeah. I guess I see what you mean. Okay. Here I am, I'll take your confession."

"I said I was joking." For a minute, the room felt hot. That window didn't let in much air.

"Of course. Sorry. Is it okay if I ask you how you are?"

I stuck my finger into the tear in the cushion and pulled out a tiny bit of the cottony stuffing.

"I'm fine. Just fine."

"Hmm. Is it okay if I say that you don't seem that way to me?"

"Is it okay if you stop asking me if everything is okay before you ask me something?"

"Fair enough."

"And anyway, you don't really know me, so how can you say if I seem fine or not?"

"It's my job."

Her job. It was her job to know if I was okay or not? I thought for a minute about Elinor Clements. Her father's job was to clothe the Big and Tall. Her mother's job was to take appointments for people's sick cats. Whose job was it to make sure Ellie made it safely from earth science to the library?

There was a long silence between us, during which I stared up at the stained-glass window and the many shades of light that it cast on the walls around us.

"I guess maybe you're right," I said. "I guess I'm not really doing all that great."

Mariah

Silas. Silas Calhoun. Silas fill-in-the-blank Calhoun. I didn't know his middle name. I made a note to myself to ask him.

SilasSilasSilasSilas. CalhounCalhounCalhounCalhoun.

We'd been talking on the phone almost every night. Whenever I called, usually around nine, he'd answer and after about an hour or so he'd ask if I wanted to talk to Emma and I'd say it was getting late and I'd better get back to my homework but we both knew that I wasn't really calling to talk to Emma anyway. I was calling to talk to Silas. He had a deep voice with soft edges and a laugh like he couldn't quite catch his breath.

We never talked about Bronwyn, but it was obvious that they were having trouble. If things were so great between them then why wasn't he on the phone with *her* for an hour every night?

The morning of the Ellie Clements story he found me in the hallway and we sat together talking on a bench. It was the first time we ever hung out together at school except for the time we went out to the hill by the athletic fields, but nobody could see us together there. When we were on the bench in the hallway, we were together for all of Odious to see.

Silas thought we should go see Detective Stevens. He said he'd tried talking to Emma about it but she refused to discuss anything at all having to do with what happened down by the river. Silas had a theory. He thought maybe the same guy who attacked Emma had something to do with Ellie's disappearance.

"I don't think so, Silas. She lived on the other side of the river. That's pretty far away from here."

"So what?"

"I don't know, this guy didn't exactly look like he drove a sports coupe."

"What are you saying?"

"Nothing really, I just mean that this guy didn't seem like the type who gets around easily."

"What, he had no legs? Don't you think you should have mentioned that to the police?"

"No, stupid. I mean, I don't know, he seemed like a vagrant, and I don't really know how someone like that would make his way thirty miles north and across the river."

"Did you tell the police that he seemed like a vagrant?"

It was time to change the subject. Silas was asking too

many questions. I knew he wanted to be a lawyer. He wanted to be like one of those lawyers on *Law & Order* or one of those legal shows I never watch because they seem kind of boring. I knew this about Silas because he'd told me that was what he wanted to do. He wanted to go to Columbia Law School after he got his undergraduate degree from Columbia.

"Settle down there, Clarence Darrow," I said.

"How do you know about Clarence Darrow?"

"Why do you seem so surprised that I'd know about Clarence Darrow? He was one of our nation's greatest lawyers. The Scopes trial? Scottsboro? C'mon, Silas, I'm not an idiot." What Silas was forgetting was that he'd told me on the phone that he wanted to be the next Clarence Darrow, and I had no idea who that was, so I looked him up on the Internet.

"I never said you were an idiot. You're just surprising, is all."

Just then we saw Emma walking down the hall and Silas jumped up like we'd been caught doing something wrong. He called out to her and waved her over but she just kept on walking.

A few days later I got a call from Detective Stevens. He wanted to meet with all of us again down at the station.

Needless to say, I didn't really want to go, but it became clear that I had no choice. My mom had already talked with Emma's and Anna's parents and they had agreed on a time. Three on Saturday. Carl was coming. Mom and Carl were going to get a sitter and spend a few precious hours away from perfect little Jessica. This was a big deal.

It seemed like a good idea for us all to get together, to go over the details of our story again, but Emma wouldn't agree to meet with us. I couldn't figure out why she was being such a bitch. At first I thought Emma was so cool and that Anna was the dud, but now it was starting to seem like I had everything backwards. Emma was sulky. She was too wrapped up in herself. It was no wonder that Owen totally blew her off after that first night at DJ's. She was turning out to be someone nobody wanted to be around.

I met Anna in the library on the Friday afternoon before our meeting down at the station. She wasn't worried at all. Mostly she wanted to talk about Tobey Endo. I was getting a little tired of that topic and also of having to convince her that she had a chance with him. Tobey was a little weird. He was cute, for sure, but he was kind of a loner and had long hair that hung in his eyes and he was always writing and sketching in this little notebook of his. He wasn't your typical Odious jock type. Maybe Anna had a chance with him. Maybe she didn't. But it seemed like telling her I thought she had a chance was the right thing to do. That's the kind of lie I'm pretty sure makes you a decent person instead of a big fat liar.

Just as we were moving on from Tobey back to the night by the river, a girl I'd never seen before walked into the library. She had long straight red hair and she wore jeans and an Indian-print shirt. New faces jump out at you in a place like this, and so does someone not in uniform. But I would have noticed her anyway because her hair was such a deep, dark shade of red and her face was so pale. She was beautiful. She carried a stack of blue flyers and pinned one to the bulletin board by the front desk; then she brought one over to our table.

"Hey, guys. Take Back the Night march over at the college. Next Friday night. Be there." Her nails were painted a color that matched her hair. She wore tan suede clogs.

I looked at the flyer. It said:

> *This is OUR world. WE make the rules.*
> *WE say that girls will be safe walking home from school.*
> *WE say that girls will be safe in our schools or on our streets or sitting by the river.*
> *WE say that girls will grow up to be women who will live without fear.*
> *Let's TAKE BACK THE NIGHT.*
> *Join us for a midnight march from the gates of the college, through the surrounding neighborhoods, down to the river and back.*
> *This is OUR world. Let's reclaim it.*
> *STOP VIOLENCE AGAINST WOMEN NOW!!!*

Anna clutched the flyer and called out to the redheaded girl, "Hey! We were there! We were there!"

I said *"Shhhhh"* and Anna shrugged and shot me a look that said *Sorry, I forgot this is a library*, but that isn't really what I meant when I shushed her.

Red-hair-and-nail girl turned around and came back to our table. "You aren't Emma Calhoun, are you?"

"No. I'm Anna. This is Mariah. We were with Emma that night."

"Hey. Wow. Heavy." She sat down. "I'm Crystal, I'm cochair of the Feminist Union and I take classes with Professor Calhoun. Pamela Calhoun, not Raymond. He's a pig. Anyway, we're having this march on Friday. We had one last month too, but we didn't veer any farther than about two blocks off campus. This time we want to march not only for the women on our campus, but also for the victims in the larger community. We're going to cut a wider swath. It'll be a long one. Bring your marching shoes."

Anna was beaming. "We'd love to go."

"Hey, that'd be great. It'll be really powerful having you along. I'm hoping that we can get some folks from Kapachuck to come down for this too, but I'm not having much luck. It's a long drive for a midnight march. And anyway, they're still too wrapped up in searching for Ellie Clements, like there's any chance she's still alive."

"Who knows," said Anna. "The police thought maybe she ran away."

"Yeah, sure," said Crystal. "Not likely." She stood up again. "Well, I gotta go. I gotta keep spreading the word."

"Oh man. This is a disaster," I said. I put my head in my hands. Anna was folding the flyer neatly and slipping it into her backpack.

"You worry too much, Mariah. This is a good thing. Lots of bad stuff happens to women on college campuses and all over. And something probably did happen to Ellie Clements. It can't hurt to get our community out in the streets demonstrating that we aren't going to let this stuff happen anymore."

I could see that she had a point, but still, I didn't feel like taking to the streets. I felt like taking to bed until this all went away.

Anna

We filled up the waiting room of the police station. With the three of us and three sets of parents, there weren't any more chairs. I stood reading the peeling posters on the walls about keeping kids off drugs and what to do if someone is choking and I tried to ignore how quiet a room filled with nine people could be.

Detective Stevens poked his head in and waved at everyone and then asked if Mariah and Emma and I could join him in his office. Emma's dad jumped up from his seat.

A few quick facts about Raymond Calhoun: He's kind of a jerk. He always corrects my grammar. He's full of himself. He's not that nice to Emma's mom. And also, and I never manage to put this out of my head whenever I'm around him, there's that stuff Emma told me about why they left the city.

"If you don't mind, I'd like to be there for this discussion," he said.

Detective Stevens stepped into the waiting room, closed the door behind him and stood with his back against it. "I'm sorry. That's not possible."

"Listen, Detective." Raymond's face was red now. "If you don't mind my saying, I don't exactly think you're doing a bang-up job with this investigation. My daughter was lucky. She made it home that night. But I don't want to take any chances. I want this guy caught and put behind bars and, frankly, I'm not sure you're up to the task."

Mariah's stepfather was on his feet now, standing next to Emma's father. I looked over at my dad. He was still sitting in the uncomfortable blue plastic chair. He smiled a sad smile at me.

"I'm sorry you feel that way, Mr. Calhoun." Detective Stevens pulled at his tie.

"Dr. Calhoun."

"Excuse me?"

"I have a doctorate in English literature."

"Oh. Okay. Fine. Whatever. Dr. Calhoun. We don't allow parents in when we interview witnesses. It can tamper with our process. I understand that you want to protect your daughters, but you have to understand that that's also what we want. That's what we do for a living. We protect people."

This seemed to work on Raymond. He took his seat again. So did Mariah's stepdad. We followed Detective Stevens down the halls of the station, through a large room with officers typing on gigantic old computers, to a door he held open for us. "We can talk in here, my boss's office."

He sat behind a big desk and we sat in chairs facing him and a nameplate that said DET. ROBERT CAPUTO. He picked up a pen and twirled it between his fingers.

"My boss wanted me to bring you guys in here again. He wanted me to find out whether there could be any connection between what happened to you and what happened up in Kapachuck. What do you guys think of that?"

Silence. Detective Stevens stared at us. He was tugging at one of his Howdy Doody ears. I hated being there. I hated the way he held that spiral notebook and the pen in his hand. I hated the way he stared at us with his wide eyes, waiting. Someone had to say something.

I was surprised to find that that person was me. "I dunno."

"Okay. Let's start over." He leaned back in his chair. He put his feet up on the desk but then he seemed to remember that it wasn't his desk and he quickly put his feet back on the floor. "What do we know about this man who attacked you?"

"Not much," I said, because I had taken on the role of Anna Who Does All the Talking.

"Well, do we think maybe he was a homeless person?"

"What? Where'd you get that idea?" I asked.

He didn't answer right away. Again, he was practicing his Detective Stevens waiting method. I glanced at Emma, who had that faraway look in her eyes she seemed to be perfecting. Mariah looked like she was doing some kind of feverish calculation in her head. Her eyes were darting back and forth.

"Let's see." He looked down at his notepad. He tapped it a few times with his pen. "Silas Calhoun." He looked at Emma. "Your brother. He told me that Mariah told him that the man appeared to be a vagrant."

I didn't say anything. I didn't remember that part of the story.

Mariah finally spoke up. "Yeah. I guess I can't be sure but he was dirty and he smelled kind of bad and his clothes were beat-up."

"Is this true?" The question was directed at Emma and me.

"Um, yeah, I guess Mariah's right. I can't remember so well but that sounds right to me," I said, because what else could I say to make Detective Stevens stop looking at me?

"Emma?" he asked.

Emma shot an angry look at Mariah. "Why are you talking about this to Silas?"

Detective Stevens didn't take his eyes off Emma. "Does this seem right? You were in the best position to say."

She stopped glaring at Mariah and turned back to Detective Stevens. "I don't really know."

"Okay. Fine. I don't want to push anything on you. But I do wish you'd told me this at the beginning, Mariah. Every detail is critically important. Is there anything else you, any of you, might be forgetting? Is there anything at all you need to tell me? If there is, please, the time to tell me is now."

"No," I said.

"No," said Mariah.

Emma didn't answer right away. She looked down at her lap. She looked like she was close to tears. I saw her jaw clench. But then, in a voice that I could barely hear, she said, "No, Detective Stevens. Unfortunately, there isn't anything I'm forgetting."

Emma

Ms. Malachy thought it was important for me to participate in the Take Back the Night march. She thought it would help me work through some of my PTSD. That stands for post-traumatic stress disorder. That's what Ms. Malachy thought I had. PTSD. She said I was putting up a wall to protect myself from the memory of what happened that night. She said I put up a wall between myself and the truth. I told her that I thought building a wall like that sounded like a perfectly reasonable thing to do.

My mom wanted me to go on the march too. Some of her students were organizing it and she thought the whole family could go together to show how grateful we were that the college students were taking what happened to me so seriously.

I agreed to go, but not for Ms. Malachy and not for my mom or her students. I wanted to march for Ellie Clements.

I remember when I was little and I used to watch Saturday-morning cartoons and Wile E. Coyote would chase the Road Runner over the edge of a cliff and he'd freeze right there, high above the rocky earth below, and as soon as he realized how high up he was, he'd fall. I thought about Ellie's family and how they were like Wile E. Coyote, perched over an abyss, staring down at a life without their daughter.

I knew that all hope of finding her alive was pretty much gone, but I liked imagining Ellie out there somewhere, using the survival skills she'd learned as a junior explorer, beating the odds. I imagined her swimming. She was an excellent swimmer. That's what the article said. But really, I knew that the dangers she faced couldn't be helped by rubbing two sticks together to make a fire or by doing a flawless butterfly stroke.

The blue flyers that littered our school all week were right: it was time to Take Back the Night. This madness had to stop.

It was also time to Take Back My Brother. I should have known that it would come to this. All this time that I thought Mariah wanted to be my friend, she really just wanted to get closer to Silas. It's always been that way. My friends have always had crushes on my brother. Just look at Anna. But it was never a serious threat until now. I'd never had a friend like Mariah. I'd never had a friend who had a way of getting exactly what she wanted. I'd been walking around in a daze thinking, me, poor me, poor me and what happened to me, and I hadn't paid any attention to what was happening around me, what was happening right in front of me.

The night of the march came and we ate dinner late so that we wouldn't get hungry while we were out walking the streets past midnight because this isn't New York City and there's nowhere to get something to eat if you get hungry after nine o'clock.

Silas came to my room while I was getting ready. I didn't know how to prepare for this night, so I reached for what felt familiar: my worn-out sneakers, my red fleece jacket, things that would make me comfortable outside on a cool spring night. I felt grateful for these simple things because inside, I was in knots, and there was nothing I could pull from my closet or from a drawer that would make that go away.

Silas sat down on my bed and asked, probably for the five hundredth time since this whole mess began, if I was okay.

"Jesus, Silas. Enough. Okay? I'm fine. Stop treating me like a child. I'm not a child. I'm not naïve. I'm not stupid. I know things."

"What are you talking about? I never said you were naïve or stupid."

I stared at him hard.

There was a hole in the knee of his pants. He wore a short-sleeved T-shirt. It was cold outside. For someone so together, Silas was pretty clueless sometimes.

Didn't he know Mariah was after him? Was he doing anything that might give her the wrong idea?

Silas brought his eyebrows together and then sighed one of his Silas sighs. I knew how worried he was about me. I hated how worried he was about me, but what could I do? For the first time in my life, I couldn't talk to Silas. I couldn't tell him the truth.

"Grab a jacket, will you? It's cold out," I said, and I walked out of my room.

The crowd was huge, gathered on the lawn in front of the main college building. I wasn't sure that I'd been in this large a crowd since I moved up here. It wasn't just Mom's students who'd shown up. There were college boys with beer on their breath. Professors in unfashionable, too-blue blue jeans. There were tons of kids from ODS because our school president, Darby O'Shea, who was there with bullhorn in hand, had decided that the ODS student council would cosponsor the march with the college's Feminist Union. Blue and gold letter jackets from Orsonville High were scattered throughout the crowd. And lots of parents were there, holding tight to their daughters' hands.

My family came in one car, but as soon as we got there my parents and my brother disappeared into the sea of people. Mom found some of her students, Dad some of the faculty, and Silas went off with Bronwyn, who at least was nice enough to come and say hello before dragging Silas away. I wandered around. I knew Anna and Mariah must be somewhere in the crowd but I made no effort to find them.

And then I saw him. There he was. He had his arm around a tall, skinny girl with short brown hair and a corduroy jacket. She was whispering something in his ear and he threw his head back and laughed and then, just at that moment, our eyes met. Somewhere deep inside, the saner part of me knew that he couldn't possibly be laughing at me, but I couldn't quite get in touch with this part of myself. I felt my face go hot. I felt my late-night dinner curdling in my stomach.

Owen nodded at me in a way that probably nobody but I would have noticed, and then he turned around and walked away, his hips knocking into the hips of that tall, skinny girl with short brown hair.

I heard a voice on a loudspeaker but I couldn't make out what it was saying over the noise of the crowd and the feedback from the microphone. I imagined it was saying, *Let's all stop and look at that loser Emma Calhoun. Isn't she pathetic?* But the voice was saying something about getting the march going, because suddenly the crowd was moving and I was swept along with it, and just as I thought that maybe I would drown, if it were actually possible to drown in a sea of people, I felt someone grab ahold of my hand. Silas.

"Let's do this," he said, and he squeezed me tight.

That night I walked probably three miles but I couldn't tell you where or how. I drifted along. When we got down to the river there was a pause. I saw Anna up at the front of the crowd. I felt Silas loosen his grip on my hand, but that only made me grab on tighter. I stayed where I was, anchored to my brother.

A college student with dark red hair faced the crowd. Her voice was hoarse from chanting. Her face was beaded with sweat. I thought, This is a march, not a race: relax. She was exploding with energy. I guess that's why she didn't need a fleece pullover like I did. She wore a black tank top with a picture of Elinor Clements on the front. Her arms were wispy and white like snow in the Arctic Circle.

She was carrying a sign that said "End the Victimization of Women NOW." I'm not sure how she knew who we were but when she found Silas and me in the crowd, she ran over to us and said, "He shouldn't be here! He should have stayed home! He should have stayed out of academia altogether!"

When she saw the puzzled look on our faces she said, "Your father. The esteemed Professor Raymond Calhoun. He doesn't belong here. Not tonight." And she marched away.

Mariah

I didn't want to go on the march. But of course Carl was on my case about going, because Carl loves nothing more in this whole wide world than to be on my case. He thought it would look strange if I didn't show up. He thought somehow somebody somewhere would pass judgment on him if I didn't go. It wasn't about me. It never is with Carl. So I lied and I told him that I was having killer cramps and that pretty much shut him up about the whole thing.

I spent the evening with Jessica. I painted her toenails a light shimmery shade of pink that I was pretty sure would go unnoticed by Carl. I told her not to tell. I made her sign an oath of secrecy. She giggled. We slipped it under her mattress. I coaxed her mop of light brown curls into a French braid. We played Candy Land and I let her win. We made popcorn and tried dyeing it purple using grape juice but that didn't work, so we threw it away and made another batch, which we devoured while watching *Mary Poppins*.

Late that night, lying in bed, with no light to see by but the red numbers on my digital alarm clock, I heard voices.

Hundreds of voices.

I threw my windows open. I could hear the marchers out in the streets. I could hear chanting and talking and hollering and even some laughter but I couldn't make out any words.

And then it hit me. They are out there because of me.

I was used to being powerless. I wound up in this big house and in that fancy private school, with a new father and sister, without ever agreeing that any of this was a good idea. But now, when I heard those voices out there in the streets, I realized that I did have power. I had the power to bring together hundreds of voices.

I closed my windows and put a pillow over my head. I tried to drown them out. I tried to make them go away. All I wanted now was quiet. I didn't want power. Power was way overrated.

I knew Anna was out there somewhere. She had agreed to show the marchers where the assault took place. I pictured them all stopped there, looking at the river, staring at the spot where Anna and Emma and I sat and made up this little story that grew and grew and grew until all these people were out in the streets when they should all have been home, in their beds, fast asleep.

I didn't want to go on the march. I didn't want to be a part of this anymore. And I didn't know what to say to Anna. Carl told me that I wasn't allowed to spend time with her. He said I had to end our friendship. He said she was bad news, a bad seed, a bad influence. Bad cliché after bad cliché. He said he wasn't spending all this money to send me to Odious so that I could hang out with the daughter of someone in the CompuCorp sales department who hadn't had a promotion in five years. He said that children of parents like that spend their time hanging out by the river, getting into trouble. He said I needed to find friends who were more like me, but then he corrected himself: I needed to find friends who came from families more like mine.

Not that any of this mattered. Since when did I listen to Carl? But it showed once again how Carl didn't know anything about anything or anyone. Especially me.

The march was all over the papers the next day. Ellie Clements's picture was on the front page along with a reference to the three minors who were involved in the assault at the riverbank, whose names were being withheld to protect their privacy, as if we had any privacy to begin with. The reporter didn't even need to talk to any of us to get our version of the story. That's how private the story had become.

The word *mobilizing* was used probably ten times in the article. Students were mobilizing. The community was mobilizing. Local government was mobilizing: there was going to be some kind of public-safety summit with all the community leaders of all the nearby towns to discuss how they should respond to the recent spate of violence. There was a quote from Detective Caputo, Detective Stevens's boss, saying that they were close to solving the Orsonville case and that they were sharing information with the squad from Kapachuck.

We are not going to sit by and let this happen to our children. We will see that justice is done.

That quote wasn't from Darby O'Shea, president of the Odious student body, or any of the members of the college Feminist Union. It didn't come from Detective Stevens or his boss, Detective Caputo. That quote, big and bold in the center of the front page of our local newspaper, came from the mayor of Orsonville.

I knew right then and there what would happen next.

The phone call came late in the afternoon, about ten days after the march.

Someone had been arrested.

Someone was going to pay.

Anna

Two major events in my life were taking place at the very same time, after a lifetime of very little in the major-event department.

First things first: I had a new relationship with Tobey Endo. All my time spent outside of school was spent instant-messaging with him. The first one came at two a.m. on the night of the march. I saw Tobey there, but we didn't talk. He was holding his skateboard in his hand and he was wearing a green and blue striped wool hat. He smiled at me and I smiled back and when I got home and turned on my laptop, I could see he was online:

sK8teR817: hey, u there?

I sat and stared at those nine letters for what felt like hours. Yes, I was there; it was finally my turn to be there.

I sent him back an IM saying only:

AnnaBanana133: yeah

And then:

**sK8teR817: u were really brave tonight Hendricks
sK8teR817: I think that's cool.**

Since then we'd talked about everything. Well, not really talked, but instant-messaged about everything. We never talked at school. We didn't have any classes together and we sat with different people at lunch. But every day I came straight home after school—I wasn't hanging out with Emma and Mariah anymore—and I went up to my room and closed the door and turned on my computer and there he was.

And through instant-messaging with Tobey, I discovered the second major event occurring in my life. It says a lot about Tobey and what he's like that he knew even before I did that David Allen had been arrested. My mom wasn't home yet that afternoon and I didn't check our voice mail and so it was Tobey who told me, because he picked something up on his scanner.

Tobey was obsessed with crime. He had a police scanner in his room that he never turned off, he just turned it down at night when he was trying to sleep. He watched all these police shows, both real, like *Cops*, and fake, like reruns of *NYPD Blue*. He wanted to be one of those people who sketch scenes they show on the news when cameras aren't allowed in the courtroom. That, and a professional skateboarder.

Tobey called me when he heard the stuff about the arrest on his scanner. Tobey IM'd me; he never called me. I saw ENDO, EUGENE on the caller ID and my hand shook as I picked up the phone.

I was so surprised and excited to hear his voice that it took a while before it hit me that someone had been arrested for a crime that I, at least in part, invented. Maybe this should have occurred to me right away, but the truth is, it didn't, and I wasn't going to feel guilty about that, especially after learning what I learned later that day about David Allen.

Mom came home from work and took me down to the police station. David Allen had been arrested, but he hadn't been charged, and a public defender had been assigned to him and was going to be present when we identified him.

He'd been picked up in Kapachuck. He was found sleeping in the woods behind a public park and when the officers asked him what he was doing there, instead of just answering, "Sleeping, what does it look like I'm doing?" he told them that he was usually down in Orsonville but that he'd come to Kapachuck because he'd heard that there was a new human-services agency that might be able to help him find a job and a place to live. Even though this turned out to be true, that there was a new agency called Family of Kapachuck, the fact that he said he was usually in Orsonville made a lightbulb go on over the arresting officer's head.

So this officer called the cops down in Orsonville, and Detective Stevens and his boss, Detective Caputo, drove up to interview David Allen and they returned with David Allen sitting in the backseat of their unmarked car wearing a pair of handcuffs.

He couldn't account for where he was on the day that Elinor Clements disappeared beyond saying that he was sleeping off too much Zima somewhere in the woods between Orsonville and Kapachuck. That wasn't much of an alibi. And when he was questioned about where he was the night that we were attacked, he stupidly said he couldn't be sure but he was probably sleeping somewhere near the banks of the Hudson River in the town of Orsonville.

I recognized him right away. I'd seen him many times. I'd seen him almost every time I went near the river, except, as it happened, on the night we said we were attacked. He always wore the same black and red plaid wool jacket and brown hiking boots. He was bearded, with a deep rust-colored tan that didn't seem to fade and a layer of dirt on his face, but beyond this, David Allen was hard to describe. He was average height, average weight, and it was hard to tell exactly how old he was. His hair wasn't brown exactly or black or gray, it was some combination of dull earthy tones.

We were asked if we had seen him before and we all said yes. And this was an absolute truth. When asked if we had seen him by the river, we all said yes. Another truth. When asked if he was the man who attacked us on that night in March when the sky was clear enough to show off its stars, we said we didn't know.

Detective Caputo took the three of us into his office. The public defender, who had short white hair, round glasses and a wrinkled suit, wanted to come in too, but Detective Caputo said no. The public defender said something about how a meeting without his client's counsel present violated some kind of rule, but Detective Caputo closed the door while he was in midsentence. Detective Stevens wasn't invited to join us either, and I could see him through the window sitting at one of the many desks in the large detective area, pretending to do paperwork, sneaking glances in our direction.

"Let me tell you what I think, ladies," Detective Caputo said. "I think this guy did something unspeakable to that poor little girl in Kapachuck. I think he did what he did, and he doesn't give a rat's ass about it. Unfortunately for us, he didn't leave behind any kind of trace of what he did. And unfortunately for the Clements girl and her family, she isn't here to point the finger at him. But luckily, you guys are here. You got away from him. We can't nail him for murder, but we can get him for assault and at least that'll get him out of our lives and off the streets for a long, long time."

He peeled the fine silvery paper off a breath mint and popped it in his mouth.

"I know these types," he continued. "I've been at this job almost thirty years now. I know a predator when I see one, and this guy's got *predator* written all over him. The signs are there. No family. A loner. A loser. Never done anything with his life. And he's got a record. A long, quite colorful record."

Images of David Allen came back to me, times I'd noticed him hanging around.

I know a predator when I see one.

I'd never really looked at him or thought about him or worried that he might cause any trouble. He just lived in the background, out of focus. Now I wondered why I'd never stopped to think that he could have been dangerous.

He's got a record. A long, quite colorful record.

"So, how 'bout it, girls?" asked Detective Caputo. "Do you think we've got our man?"

I looked at my hands in my lap. They looked small and weak.

"Let me try this again," he said. "You've all seen him before, right?"

We nodded. Yes.

"He hangs out by the river?"

More nodding.

"Now, I'm thinking . . . he fits the description. He's average size. No distinguishing features. It was dark, so you couldn't see his face, I understand that. But it all fits. He's a vagrant. He frequented the river. So, I'll ask again, do you think maybe he's the guy who attacked you that night?"

Mariah spoke first. "I don't know . . . I don't think so."

"But can you rule him out? Can you say for certain that it wasn't him?"

She paused. "Well . . . no . . . I guess I can't rule him out for certain . . . but . . ."

"How about you, can you rule him out?"

He was asking me.

I wanted this to end. I wanted to leave this office and go back to my life and my school and my new table at lunchtime and IM'ing Tobey.

This guy David Allen was trouble. He was a predator. He had a record. He probably did have something to do with Ellie Clements, at least that was what Detective Caputo thought, and I figured he must know more than any of us about these things.

I took in a breath of the stale air. "No," I said. "I can't rule him out."

We all turned to Emma. She started to say something, but then she stopped. She cupped her hands over her eyes, but I could see from where I was sitting that under her interlocking fingers her eyes were squeezed shut. Her face was flushed. She sighed, and she shook her head slowly back and forth.

"Well then," said Detective Caputo. "I guess that's enough for me."

Emma

Here's something else I learned about Ellie Clements from reading about her. She had an older brother. He wasn't mentioned in any of the early articles, but once the stories about her started to read more like obituaries than calls for help, more of the details of her life came out.

I hoped he was kind to her. I hoped he didn't get annoyed when she came knocking at the door to his room and that he let her borrow his things. I hoped he stayed home on some weekend nights to watch movies with her. I hoped he took her somewhere sometimes, just the two of them, so they could talk, or sit quietly side by side on a train with the river on their left.

Ms. Malachy asked me how I felt about the arrest of David

Allen. I was tired of being asked how I felt about things. Those were questions I didn't know how to answer. I'd lost most of my senses. I didn't taste food. I couldn't smell the fresh-cut grass in the school quad. And I didn't feel anything about David Allen. I didn't feel happy. I didn't feel relieved. I didn't feel "closure," which was something Ms. Malachy said she was hoping I would feel. I just felt that white expanse of nothingness slowly spreading to the edges of me.

"Is there something else going on?" she asked me. She was wearing a blue bandana in her hair and an Ecuadorian wool sweater even though her office felt hot, like it must feel at the equator, which made me wonder why they knit so many of those heavy wool sweaters in Ecuador.

"Not really."

"How are things at home?"

"I guess they're like they always are." She stared at me. She needed more. "By which I mean they're fine."

I don't think I sounded very convincing. The truth was things weren't so great at home. After the march, after that girl with the red hair said those things about my father, after she gathered some of her friends and starting chanting, "Hey, ho, Raymond Calhoun has got to go," after their voices rose above the crowd and people stopped to stare, after the school paper wrote about my father the next week and how he'd been given "safe haven" at the college after sexually harassing students at his previous job, things had been a little tense at home.

It even seemed to be getting to Silas. I had come home one day and it was just Dad and Silas in the kitchen and when

I walked in, Silas stormed out. Silas is not a stormer. He never has been. Dad looked at me and shrugged. I went to Silas's room but he didn't answer the door when I knocked. I paced up and down the hall for a few minutes and then went back to the kitchen to talk to Dad, but he was gone.

"What about your friends? Anything new there?" Ms. Malachy asked.

"I don't really have time for my friends right now."

"Really? What are you busy with?"

"Stuff."

"Hmmm. Stuff. Do you have a boyfriend?"

The picture of Owen knocking his hips into the hips of the tall, skinny girl with short brown hair came back to me. Touch, step. Touch, step. Touch, step. That is how they walked away, in sync with the loud beating of my heart.

I opened my mouth to say "No, of course not," but my words got caught in my throat. They lingered on my tongue. I couldn't spit them out. Like everything else, I couldn't even taste them.

"So there is somebody," she said.

I stared at the design on her sweater. Interlocking brown and red diamonds with white trim. If you go to Ecuador and you go to the equator and you stand perfectly still, right on the line that divides the earth in two, at certain times in the year you have no shadow.

"Tell me about him."

Touch, step. Touch, step. Touch, step. And there was the laughter. The way they shared something, a whisper, something that had a meaning only between the two of them.

"His name is Owen," I began. "And he isn't my boyfriend."

He whispered things to me too. I felt his hot breath in my ear, back when I could feel things. "I had sex with him."

Silence.

"Wow. That's a pretty important event. Sharing that part of yourself with somebody."

"I guess so."

"So where is he now? What happened between you?"

"Nothing really. It just wasn't . . . it just didn't work out."

"And you're okay with that?"

"Sure."

"What was it like?"

I started to feel something. A little trickle of a feeling. I took a deep breath. Closed my eyes. Willed it to stop.

I smiled at her. "I'm sure you must know what it's like having sex."

"That's not what I mean, Emma, and I think you know that."

I looked at the clock. The minute hand had completed its full rotation. A perfect circle, like the earth. Our time was up.

Mariah

David Allen. Weren't guys like this, guys who got arrested for attacking young girls, supposed to have three names? Like David Allen Smith. Or maybe David Smith Allen. David Allen sounded like only part of a name. Like something had been cut away. Like something was missing.

I couldn't stop thinking about him, sitting alone in his cell. DavidDavidDavidDavid. AllenAllenAllenAllen.

More than anything, it just seemed like a lousy time of year to be locked up inside. It was May. Perfect weather. Not too hot. No rain. The river was swollen and the banks were lush with green, lavender, orange and yellow. I stood by the rushing water one day after school and smelled the air and watched a dragonfly, and it was as if, with the end of May, the clouds had been lifted away. They no longer hung low above our school, our town, or our community of concerned citizens. Darby O'Shea, Detective Caputo, even the mayor, had declared this chapter over. The world was safe again.

Except for one nagging little piece of truth: David Allen was nowhere near us the night of the attack. Or, I should say, the night we said we were attacked. We said we were attacked. We weren't. There was no attacker. No staring evil in the face. No man with a knife who wasn't afraid to use it. No David Allen. Only a ghost we conjured out of the clear night air, a ghost we hoped would protect us.

Two things kept me from going to Detective Stevens with the truth. Well, maybe three things. I'll take the first two first. One: a prison cell is a home, even if not the ideal one. Four walls. A roof. A bed. Three meals a day. David Allen had none of this before his arrest. Lame, I know, but this was a lie I told myself to make things easier. Two: David Allen had a record. Elinor Clements was missing. The cops were probably right. He was probably the one who snatched her away. Keeping him off the streets would keep other girls on the streets.

I have to confess that the third thing that kept me from going to Detective Stevens was that I'm a big fat coward. I was afraid of what would become of us, of me, if we did tell the truth about that night. We were beyond grounding, beyond no phone, no TV, no allowance, don't leave your room for a month, you're going to boarding school. I didn't need to be Clarence Darrow to know that we had probably committed a crime. And I wasn't ready to cop to that. This was over. Wrapped up neatly and tucked away. Now David Allen had a bed and four walls and a roof over his head and I could have my life back.

Silas and Bronwyn broke up. He got into Columbia like everyone knew he would and she was going to Smith College, which is all women, and why anyone would want to go to an all-women school made absolutely no sense to me. Smith happened to be just a few hours away from New York City, but it might as well have been light-years away, because Silas decided he didn't want to have a girlfriend at another school. I knew this was coming. I knew he didn't love her the way he used to. I know these things about people. I pride myself on it. I'd learned some valuable lessons since my time with DJ. I can tell when there's an imbalance of love and affection between two people. Like, for instance, with Mom and Carl. He may be an asshole, but he worships her, and for that, she likes him just fine.

I could tell it was over with Bronwyn by the way Silas talked to me, and the way he always managed to catch my eye in the hallway and touch my arm or shoulder as I passed by. He was using this Smith College excuse just to let her down gently, which just goes to show you how sensitive a guy Silas Calhoun is.

He found me after school; he was lurking by my locker and he asked if I wanted a ride home. I said sure and he said, "Great. I'll meet you at the corner of Spruce and McDonnell." He flashed me a quick smile and then disappeared in the crowd of Odious students, all fighting their way out the doors for a taste of the sweet freedom that comes every day at three.

The corner was only a few blocks from the main gate to

campus and I didn't mind the walk because the day was perfect, but it seemed kind of foolish to walk to Spruce and McDonnell because that basically cut in half the distance between school and my house. I hardly needed a ride, but I was pretty sure that wasn't what Silas was offering.

He was waiting for me in his black Honda Civic. I threw my bag in the backseat, which I noticed was cramped and cluttered. He was listening to the college radio station's jazz hour. The car smelled like bubble gum.

"How about a cup of coffee?" he asked.

"Sounds perfect."

I assumed he'd head toward the Big Cup, but instead he turned onto the parkway and started driving north. The trees on either side of the road were full and created a big leafy tunnel that we drove through in near silence, with just some piano chords and the *dlum dlum* of a stand-up bass, and I didn't ask where we were going. I kind of hoped we'd drive all day and all night, out of Orsonville, past Kapachuck, away from the river, away from ghosts, across the New York border into Canada and beyond.

But Silas pulled off in Greenfield, the small town you hit just after leaving Orsonville, and he parked at the Greek Corner, a shabby-looking diner. We ordered two plain coffees, and he got a grilled corn muffin. The booth was small and our knees almost touched under the table.

"I'm confused," he finally said to me. "And I don't know who else I can talk to about this other than you."

"So here I am." I opened a small plastic creamer and dumped it in my coffee. The white disappeared in the thick black sludge. "You talk. I'll listen." I looked up and caught him staring at me and the intensity in his eyes made me feel dizzy.

"I was hoping this was just a passing thing. I was hoping it would go away by now."

I moved my fingers across the table so they were almost touching his. He slid his the last few centimeters.

Contact.

"They've gone and caught this guy and still, Emma isn't herself. Something is wrong with her and I don't know how to fix it."

He pulled his hand away and ran his fingers through his hair. I stirred my coffee slowly and watched as it turned from thick black sludge to a muddy, murky brown.

Anna

Tobey wanted to know everything. What's it like to be questioned by the police? To identify a suspect? Was I going to testify? Would there be a trial? How did I feel when I saw him? Did I want to kill him? Could I forgive him?

I decided to do something I never do. I decided to take the first step. I decided I was done waiting, done being a follower.

I asked Tobey if he wanted to do something sometime.

I can't imagine what that would feel like, in those few seconds of waiting for an answer, if you had to ask a boy you liked face to face if he wanted to do something sometime. Waiting for a typed response, watching a flashing cursor, a blank page, was torture enough. I forgot to breathe.

sK8teR817: sure

Relief came like a cool rain falling on me. I stood up from my desk and opened my window. It was hot in my room and I wanted to take my time responding. I adjusted my pink and white curtains and thought about how it was time to redo my bedroom in more grown-up colors. I stared for a moment across the street at my neighbors' empty house. I came back to my computer screen to find:

sK8teR817: the river? Saturday at 4?

It wasn't exactly what I had in mind. I was thinking a movie, a cup of coffee, maybe hanging out at his house if his parents were out, not going down to the one place in the world I wanted to forget. But the first-step-taking, outgoing Anna was done for the day, so I just wrote:

AnnaBanana133: sure, see u there

This date with Tobey or whatever it was put me in an awkward position with my parents. I'd taken a silent oath to always tell the truth and never lie to them, but could I really tell them that I was going to meet a boy from school? Even if I could, even if that would be okay with them, even if they could finally acknowledge that I was growing up, I most definitely couldn't tell them that I was meeting him down by the river.

I decided to tell them I was meeting a boy from class (not exactly true as I have no classes with him, but kind of true since he is in the ninth grade with me) to go over some homework (who's to say we wouldn't talk about homework?) at the Big Cup (who's to say we wouldn't end up at the Big Cup after hanging out by the river?). They just smiled and said, "Fine, but go easy on the caffeine and make sure you're home by eight-thirty." That's when it gets dark here at the end of May.

I didn't know what I should wear. I felt like calling Emma. I wanted to tell her that I was going to meet Tobey and that I didn't know what to wear or what to say or what to do. But I wasn't talking to Emma. She was all wrapped up in herself and didn't seem to have any interest in being my friend anymore, and she also didn't seem to be friends with Mariah, so I had no idea who her friends were, or what she did with her time, other than spending it doing everything she could to avoid me. I missed her, but only as much as you can miss someone who you know doesn't miss you too.

I knew she was going through some stuff. It couldn't have been easy for her to have that crowd around her yelling about what a big perv her dad is. I tried. I called her the morning after the march to talk, to tell her that I was here if she needed me. She never called me back.

I picked up the phone to call Mariah, but then I decided that I didn't need anybody's help. I could do this on my own. I could figure out what to wear when meeting a boy on a Saturday afternoon down by the river. Not a skirt. Nothing too dressy. But no running shoes either. No baggy T-shirts. I settled on a pair of green Capri pants, some black platform sandals and a black scoop-neck shirt. I put my hair up in a ponytail.

Tobey was waiting for me when I arrived. He was riding his skateboard on the sidewalk and he did a jump off the curb when he saw me and then flipped the board up into his hands. I wondered if he was showing off.

"Hey, Hendricks! What's with the book bag?"

I'd left the house with it to keep up appearances for the sake of my parents.

"I'm coming from the library," I lied.

"Cool."

We stood there staring at each other. Seconds ticked by. A minute? Two? Where was the bold instant-messager who'd suggested this outing? I wished she would speak up.

He looked down at his feet. He kicked a rock in the direction of the river.

"So, if you wouldn't mind . . . would you show me where this all happened? The night of the march the crowd was pretty thick—I was stuck way in the back."

"Right over there." I pointed to the spot where Mariah and Emma and I were sitting the night we made up the story, when it was only the three of us and the river, the night we were terrified of getting in trouble with our parents for lying about being at DJ's house. From where I stood, in the warm sunlight of a Saturday afternoon in May, I looked back at that night and tried to remember why it felt like such a big deal to get caught in that lie. All things considered, the lie about being at a movie when we were really at DJ's was pretty small. There would have been consequences, for sure. But by now it would have been over and done with.

"Where did he come from?"

"We're not really sure."

Tobey looked down the river. He looked up the river. He put his hand up over his eyes to block out the sun, searching the horizon for something, maybe a sign of some kind, or a clue, some evidence the police might have overlooked. He took his notebook out of his pocket, scribbled something in it, and then seemed to give up and sat down on a rock and motioned for me to sit next to him.

"Poor Hendricks," he said. He swung his arm around my neck and gave my ponytail a playful tug. "It really sucks that this happened to you, but at least it all turned out okay." He paused. "Well, for you anyway."

I sat perfectly still. I was afraid that if I talked or breathed or even blinked my eyes, this moment would end.

"It's a good thing they caught that guy and that he's locked away because I swear, if I ever saw him, I'd seriously kick his ass."

No one had ever offered to do anything like that for me before. A huge grin spread across my face, out of my control.

"You look thirsty, Hendricks. Do you want to go get something to drink at the Big Cup?"

See. We were going to be at the Big Cup. That's the thing about lies. You never know if they just might end up becoming true.

Emma

I had sex with him. Somehow saying those words out loud to Ms. Malachy made it real. I knew this was true, I was there, and sure, I was drunk, but not so drunk that I didn't know it was happening, and yet it didn't seem real.

I don't know why I told Ms. Malachy. I hadn't told anyone. Ms. Malachy's sneaky that way; she can get you to tell her things you don't even tell your best friends, or things you don't even admit to yourself. But now the secret was out there in the world, or at least, floating around her little stuffy office, and I couldn't take it back. I couldn't preserve it in ice. It was alive. It flew around me like a gnat, buzzing annoyingly in my ear.

I thought about the way he nodded at me the night of the march. That slight movement of his head. There was an infinite world of meaning in that motion. Sometimes I thought it meant "Thank you for the special night we shared." Sometimes I thought it meant "Thank you for keeping your mouth shut in front of my tall, skinny girlfriend with short brown hair and hips that knock into mine as we walk." And sometimes I thought maybe I imagined the nod altogether.

Mostly, I tried going back to not thinking about it, or him, at all, and that wasn't too hard. I was getting pretty good at not thinking about things I'd rather not think about. I was an expert, really. The champion of nonthinking. If there were some kind of medal or award, I'd be the one up onstage, accepting it.

You wouldn't think sand castles were any kind of scientific mystery, would you? But up until very recently, physicists couldn't explain what made them work. Now they've learned that water holds sand together by forming tiny liquid bridges between dry grains, creating tension strong enough to support a structure.

But no matter how soundly you build your sand castle, there are still things like wind and rain and the tide that will break these bridges apart, and in time, your sand castle will fall.

Silas and Bronwyn broke up. I watched them and their life fade away. The apartment a short walk from Central Park, demolished. Goodbye, kids. Dog. Important jobs and fashionable clothes. Dinner parties and theater. Visits from Aunt Emma. Gone.

I wondered, briefly, if this had anything to do with Mariah. Since she didn't come over to see me anymore, her contact with Silas was cut off. She wouldn't dare talk to him at school. Not in front of Bronwyn or any of the other senior girls. That left nothing. When else could she see Silas? No, Mariah was not a factor. She wasn't an unexpected tidal wave. Mariah was stuck out at sea, bobbing around, treading water. Silas and Bronwyn were stronger than Mariah, but not strong enough to withstand the natural erosion that comes along with things like graduation and going away to school.

The college was out for the summer. The students had packed up their cars, driven one hundred miles or three thousand miles back to the rooms they'd slept in when they were still children. Mom had a two-week lecturing gig at Oxford that was apparently very prestigious, and Dad had planned to go with her. The idea was that Silas and I would stay home and finish out the school year, and they'd be back in time for his graduation. But Dad decided to stay. He wasn't going with Mom and I took this to mean that maybe their future was made out of sand too.

I was seeing Ms. Malachy weekly. I saw her during my free period on Tuesdays and nobody knew. It felt strange sneaking off to see Ms. Malachy and revealing my secrets to her when she herself was one of the biggest secrets in my life.

"I'm in therapy."

I tried saying that to myself, out loud in the shower when I knew no one was listening, and even then I wanted to look over my shoulder to make certain I wasn't heard. Therapy was something that other people did. Other people with problems.

After the Tuesday when I told Ms. Malachy I'd had sex with Owen, I skipped my appointment. I spent my free period alone, in the library, reading a back issue of *Scientific American*. The library was a ghost town. Everyone was outside; they'd given up on books. Summer was too close. There was studying to be done, notes to be reviewed, but that could happen outdoors, barefoot, sitting in clusters, surrounded by friends.

I read the same sentences over and over again.

When we're awake, different parts of the brain communicate constantly across the entire neural network. In the deepest part of sleep, however, the various nodes of your cranial nervous system lose all their connections.

The silence of the library was distracting. I could hear the humming of the air conditioner and the buzzing of the fluorescent overhead lights. Mr. Frank, the librarian, was typing something into the computer.

. . . In the deepest part of sleep, however, the various nodes of your cranial nervous system lose all their connections.

Suddenly someone was sitting across from me. Ms. Malachy. She must have had superpowers beyond just the power to sniff out secrets.

"What are you doing?"

I held up the magazine.

She nodded. "You know, it's Tuesday."

"Yeah. I know."

"It's okay to feel like taking a break. Talking can be difficult."

"Uh-huh." I started flipping through the pages of the magazine, pretending to be searching for something.

"But I also know that when you feel like taking a break, that's probably when we're getting somewhere."

She slipped off her sandals and tucked her feet underneath her. This seemed totally inappropriate to me. No shirt, no shoes, no service.

"I'm going to tell you something, Emma. I sometimes avoid things that are difficult too. Even in my role as a counselor. I let things slide by because I'm afraid of losing my students. I'm afraid if I push something difficult, that come the next week I'll be sitting at my desk staring at an empty couch. Sometimes that couch is empty anyway, even when I don't say what's on my mind. When that happens it's because the student with whom I'm meeting knows that the difficult stuff is right there, about to be unmasked, even if I'm not the one to pull the mask off it."

I stared at her hard. "What are you talking about?" I asked, even though I knew.

"Last week, I let you tell me that everything at home was fine, and I didn't mention to you that I'm aware of what's gone on with your father at the college. I let you tell me that what happened with you and this boy Owen was no big deal, when I know this can't be true. I let you tell me that the arrest of David Allen meant nothing to you. I know these things weigh on you heavily, I can see that on your face and in the way you carry yourself, and I wanted to tell you I'm sorry. I'm sorry I wasn't honest. It's not right for me to pretend around you when all I ask of you is that you don't do the same to me."

I closed the magazine. I looked up and I judged the distance between my chair and the door to the sun-drenched outside to be about fifteen steps, yet even with my head sending my legs the command, they wouldn't move. Like in sleep, there was something interfering with the connections in my brain, and it had been there, I realized, for a while now.

Mariah

The ghost we invented to protect us that night had now returned to haunt me.

I thought about David Allen all the time. I imagined a cell for him with warm light, soft music, Egyptian cotton sheets on his plush king-size bed and gourmet home-cooked meals. I created this world for him knowing this wasn't what it looked like inside a jail cell, but I wanted him to have these comforts. I wanted him to have a vacation from the cold hard world of homelessness. I wanted these things for him even though, I had to remind myself, he was the one who had kidnapped and killed Elinor Clements.

David Allen couldn't be charged with the crime of taking Elinor away from her family and friends (no body, no evidence), but they seemed to have arrived at some place that began to resemble peace, or at least acceptance. She was finally memorialized. A small local park was named in her honor. Kids at her school wore pink rubber bracelets with her name stamped on them.

I felt divided in two, which was not entirely new for me. There was the Mariah from Dexter County who lived in a tiny apartment, and the Mariah who lived in the Dalrymple house with its never-ending hallways and its black-bottomed swimming pool. There was the Mariah who everybody at Odious thought I was—stuck-up, bitchy, tough, cool—and the Mariah I really was: none of those things. And now there was the Mariah who hated David Allen and wanted to see him in pain, and the Mariah who felt sorry for him and wished he had Egyptian cotton sheets.

My mom thought I needed a break this summer and tried talking me into a camp in California. I could see Carl's fingerprints all over that plan. They'd go off on a cruise together while I went to some stupid camp. I refused to go, even though I briefly considered going and then ditching the camp and spending my time searching the streets of Los Angeles for my real father. Then I remembered that I'd invented the idea that my father worked as an actor in Los Angeles, much the same way I'd invented this cell for David Allen with soft light and gourmet meals and fancy sheets. And I decided that lately, I'd had more than my fair share of ghosts. I just wanted to spend the summer at home, living my life and hanging out with Silas as much as possible.

He had a job lined up at the bookstore on Grand and I'd

applied for a job there too. I also applied for a job at the garden center and the stationery store, neither of which excited me. What I really wanted to do, almost as much as I wanted to work with Silas at the bookstore, was to work in a homeless shelter, but I didn't even bring that up to Mom or Carl because, given the circumstances, I knew they'd look at me like I'd gone crazy.

Silas was having a rough time. Emma was still moping around and I knew things between Silas and me wouldn't really start happening until he stopped worrying about her, or at least until he accepted that she wasn't his responsibility. But there was something sweet about his obsession with Emma, and it made me want to be a better big sister to Jessica, so I started taking her out one afternoon a week for ice cream sundaes. This scored big points with Mom, who dropped the whole summer-camp-in-California idea.

I never had any intention of following Carl's rule about not spending time with Anna anymore, but somehow it happened anyway. She always went home right after school. She sat with Tammy Frost and her crowd at lunch and I didn't have any interest in that table of people at all. But the more David Allen haunted me, the more I felt the pull toward Anna and Emma, and since Emma had made it very clear that she didn't want to be my friend anymore, I called up Anna and invited her over.

It was a Sunday, and even though summer hadn't officially started, it was hot and humid. Carl was off at a conference for the weekend and Mom was delighted that I'd invited someone to the house because this wasn't something I made a habit of doing. I guess she'd forgotten about Carl's ban on all things Anna.

She brought her bathing suit and Mom made us a pitcher of mint lemonade and we sat on the striped lounge chairs and watched Jessica do handstands and retrieve rubber rings from the bottom of the deep end. Finally Mom called Jessica into the house—she thought Jessica had had enough sun and chlorine—and told her it was time to have a peanut butter sandwich and watch *Finding Nemo*. Anna and I were alone.

"So what have you been up to lately?" I asked. We both had on sunglasses and she was in a stretched-out blue Speedo one-piece that wasn't exactly flattering.

She turned to me, pushed her glasses up and shot me a huge smile. "Okay. Promise you won't tell anyone?"

"Uh . . . sure."

"I mean it. Promise for real. It's a secret."

What would ever have made her think I wasn't good at keeping secrets?

"Okay. I promise."

She took a sip of her lemonade. "It's just like you said. As soon as I stopped thinking that he was out of my league, it happened, and now I'm with Tobey Endo."

"You are?"

"Don't sound so surprised."

"No, I mean, that's great. I had no idea. But why the secret?"

"That's just the way it is with us. We IM and we hang out

sometimes on weekends but we don't really want everyone to know at school because then you have to deal with all the gossip and stuff and who wants to deal with that?" She squirted some sunblock onto her thighs and started rubbing it in.

"Wow. You and Tobey. That's great, Anna, really."

I had a feeling I was supposed to ask her more but I couldn't think of a single question, so I just cut to the reason I'd invited her here in the first place.

"I've been thinking a lot about David Allen."

"Pervert."

"What?"

"Not you, moron, him. He is so gross. Ew." She shivered. "I'm so glad he's gone and I don't have to see him again. Tobey says he'll probably plead guilty and take a lighter sentence to avoid a trial, so thank God we won't have to go to court."

"But, Anna, he didn't do it. Doesn't that bother you?"

"Not really. Look what he did to Elinor Clements."

"We don't know that for sure."

"Yes we do. Who else could it have been?"

"Anybody!"

I was shouting now. I hadn't planned on having this fight with Anna. I hadn't anticipated that I'd take the position that David Allen hadn't hurt Elinor Clements, but suddenly it was the only argument that made any sense to me.

"What do you know, Mariah? You think you know more than the police?"

"Of course I do. I know that David Allen didn't attack us

that night. The police don't know that, but I know that. And so do you."

"This is stupid. Let's just forget about it. Please. It's over."

She pushed her glasses back down onto her face so I couldn't see her eyes.

"It's over," she said, and she turned her back on me.

Anna

When Mom told me that Detective Stevens was stopping by after dinner I told her no. I guess maybe I was more forceful than I usually am with Mom because she took a step back and looked at me funny.

"What's wrong, honey?" she asked.

"Nothing. I'm just done with this. That's all. I have nothing left to say."

She pulled me into a hug. She smelled a little like the onions she'd been cutting in the kitchen. I pushed her away.

"Listen, Anna, I know you want to bury this. I know the school year is almost over and summer is here and that makes a great time for a fresh start. I want you to have that too. But if Detective Stevens needs your help, you owe him that."

"What can I possibly do for him? They've already got David Allen. Case closed."

"I don't know, dear, but I told him he could stop by. I've made an apple crumble."

"Yippee."

She looked a little hurt, but I wasn't in the mood for babysitting my mother. I went up to my room and closed the door. I turned on my computer.

AnnaBanana133: hey
sK8teR817: hey Hendricks, wats up
AnnaBanana133: Det. Stevens is coming over soon (dunno why)
sK8teR817: maybe theres a break in the case
AnnaBanana133: ???
sK8teR817: new evidence or something
AnnaBanana133: yeah, i guess so
sK8teR817: i wanna hear about it after
AnnaBanana133: cool

I didn't say much during dinner. I thought about Tobey, sitting in his room in front of his computer, the police scanner buzzing with static in the background. I thought about his striped wool hat that he wore even in the heat and the curls of sandy brown hair that poked out the bottom of it. I thought about the way his lips had felt when he'd kissed me. Or I guess I should say, when I'd kissed him. After we'd had our coffees at the Big Cup, he walked me part of the way home. The sky was electric, it was just about to get dark, the streetlamps hadn't gone on yet, and standing in front of a big brown stucco house with yellow and white striped awnings, I leaned over and put my arms around his neck and started kissing him. He seemed surprised at first, and so was I, but then he just went with it and we stood like that, kissing until the dark blue sky was turning black and I knew I was pushing my luck and I'd better get home. I thought maybe that kiss would change what it was like between us at school, but it didn't. I guess we just made more sense through IM and outside of ODS.

Dad was in the middle of talking about work and I was pretending that I was listening when the doorbell rang. Detective Stevens wasn't in uniform. He was wearing jeans and black basketball shoes and a gray hooded sweatshirt. With his short hair and his ears that stuck out and his big smile, he almost seemed like he could be a boy coming over to pick me up for a date, if that were the kind of thing that happened to me. He turned down my mom's offer of some apple crumble and I felt a twinge of embarrassment for her. He asked if my parents minded if he talked to me alone and they said no. He'd already explained why he didn't want parents around when he interviewed witnesses, but still, I was suddenly desperate to stay at the dinner table. I was glued to the seat. I made a vow to listen to Dad and take an interest in his work, but they both looked at me like *Get up, what are you waiting for?* and so I had no choice but to stand and follow Detective Stevens out the kitchen door. We sat on the back steps underneath an exposed lightbulb with moths flittering around it.

"How's the school year wrapping up?" he asked.

"Fine." He looked different out of uniform. I noticed his face for the first time. He had gray eyes and freckled cheeks and slightly crooked teeth. He wrapped his arms around his knees and pulled them to his chest.

"I'm not even really supposed to be here," he said.

"So why are you here?" I didn't mean to sound harsh, but that apple crumble was sounding good now and I just wanted to go back inside and have dessert with my parents and then go to my room and IM Tobey. I wanted Detective Stevens to go away.

"What I mean is, Detective Caputo kind of took this case away from me. He's busy getting things ready for the DA and I have some new assignments and I have tons of work to do on those cases and yet I can't stop thinking about this case, about you and Emma and Mariah."

"We're fine. We're all fine now. Don't worry about us."

He looked at me. "I'm not even on duty."

I wasn't sure what to say to that. My stomach growled.

"There are some things that just bother me. They nag at me constantly, even when I'm working on my other cases."

This was my chance to say something like "What bothers you, Detective Stevens?" but I remained silent. An agitated cricket was chirping from under something in the darkness.

"Like, for example," he continued, "did he bleed?"

"What?"

"You hit him in the head with a rock, right? Hard enough to stun him?" I couldn't just keep looking into the night. His eyes were on me. I turned to him. I nodded. "The thing about the head is, it's a messy bleeder. Lots of blood vessels close to the surface of the skin. But there was no blood anywhere at the scene. Not on any rock. Or the ground."

I shrugged.

"You know what's even harder to understand?" Pause. "Why David Allen doesn't have even the slightest sign of a cut or a bruise or any kind of trauma whatsoever to his head."

"That is strange, kind of," I said. I untied and then retied my shoelace just to keep my eyes engaged in something other than staring blankly at him. "But hasn't it been, like, two months? I guess maybe the head heals quickly."

"Not in my experience." He bent his head over and gestured to the back of it. "I was a reckless kid. Accident-prone. Always getting stitches. You can still see my scars."

I could see one through his crew cut, an inch or two in length.

"That's just from when my brother lost his grip on his tennis racket." He sat up again. "And there's something else."

I was grateful for the cricket now. It was drowning out the pounding of my heart.

"Everyone seems to recognize David Allen. They don't know his name or anything, but they've all seen him before. He was some kind of fixture down at the river. Most kids I talked to said he was always there."

Was it only one cricket? It was starting to sound like thousands.

"If that's so, then why didn't you recognize him that night? How did you not know someone you've seen before?"

"We told you. It was dark. We couldn't see. We were scared. We panicked. And anyway, why are you doing this? Why are you questioning me? What about Emma and Mariah?"

"Oh, I was planning on talking to them too. But I thought

I'd start with you because you just seem so together to me. And also, I know you're a good kid. I can tell these things."

"But I told you—"

"I know, I know, it was dark. You were scared. You panicked." He stood up. He cast a long shadow that stretched down the steps and disappeared into the backyard. "Good night, Anna."

Emma

I had tests to study for. I had a paper to write. School would be over in two weeks and I would watch Silas walk down the aisle in his black robe and his stupid square hat with the tassel and I was already imagining my future without him. There was too much going on for me to take a day off and spend it with Dad, but he insisted. He demanded. When Dad gets that way you can't say no.

He wanted to go to the racetrack. I just loved that as an excuse for why I missed a whole day of classes. Sorry I ditched school, Principal Glasser, but I was busy betting on the ponies.

This was something Dad and I had done together every summer for the first few years we'd lived up here. We would drive the hour and a half north and he would spot me twenty dollars to bet on the horses with names I liked: Proud Princess,

Jellybean, Flower Power. The odds meant nothing to me; I placed my bets solely on what sounded closest to the name I might have given my own horse at the age of eight, nine or ten. I usually lost, but a few times I won big—well, as big as you can win on a two-dollar bet. I used to love these days with Dad. We'd listen to the sound track of *West Side Story* and sing at the top of our lungs with the windows rolled down and we'd buy root beer floats at the Frosty Freeze off the highway on the way back home. But Dad's new car only had a CD player and we'd thrown away our cassette of *West Side Story* after we found it under the seat, strangled in its own tape ribbon, when Dad sold his old car. This day seemed like a terrible idea.

I insisted on bringing my books even though reading in a moving car makes me want to hurl. Dad knows this about me. That's probably why he didn't fight me on it. He knew I'd end up zipping them back into my bag.

We were listening to Bach's cello concertos. Not exactly something to roll the windows down and sing along to, but the mellow music and the green trees speeding by outside my window had a hypnotic effect on me. Just as I was settling into this rare moment of peace and nothingness, Dad pounced.

"We need to talk, Emma."

We. Need. To. Talk. Four words you never want to hear your parents say.

"Is this about you and Mom?"

This seemed to catch him off guard. He adjusted his sun visor. He fiddled with the volume knob on the stereo until it wound up exactly where it had been before he started to fiddle with it.

"Well, in a sense, yes, a bit indirectly, I suppose it is." He cleared his throat. "I wanted to talk to you about what happened the night of that march and about the article in the college paper I'm pretty sure you managed to get your hands on. All this business about the sexual harassment charges. It's time we clear this up."

Signs were approaching and then disappearing behind me. I couldn't see them. Couldn't make any sense of them. What does it mean when there's a Soft Shoulder Ahead?

"You don't have to do this, Dad."

"I know I don't have to, I want to."

"But I'm not sure I want you to. Sometimes maybe it's better not to know certain things." That sounded smarter than anything I'd ever said in all my life.

He took a deep breath, considered me for a minute and then pressed on. "Do you know what sexual harassment is?"

"I have a feeling you're going to tell me." I was glad we were driving, glad for the excuse to look straight ahead and avoid his eyes.

"I'm not really all that sure myself. The exact definition is malleable. What I do know is that one of my former students, a graduate student, made such an accusation against me and I haven't been able to shake it even after all these years."

"Was it true?"

"No."

I looked at him. He stared hard at the road. His cheeks were red. His hair was a bit of a mess from running his fingers through it. I felt like I was looking at him, really looking at him, for the first time in a long while, and what I saw made me want to grab hold of the wheel and turn the car around.

He wasn't telling the truth.

"You're lying," I said before I could stop myself. I should have let him lie. I didn't want to know the truth. I'd just told him I didn't want to know the truth. And yet here I was, putting him on the spot.

He looked over at me and his eyes were soft. His body loosened. He slunk down into his seat. He let something go.

"I'm not lying, Emma. But the truth is too complicated to explain to you. You're still too young to understand."

I turned the music off. Those cello concertos were getting to me. They were sad and hollow and they made me want to cry.

"What you need to know, Emma, is that I made a mistake and I paid for it dearly. When it became clear to me that all I cared about in this world was your mother and our family, I tried to get myself out of a situation I never should have been in in the first place. And when I tried to do that, this student of mine wanted to hurt me, and she did it in the only way she knew how, by accusing me of things that weren't true, or really, I guess what she did was put some true things into an untruthful context."

Maybe a Soft Shoulder is what happens to you when you are beaten down and defeated and you give up on keeping up appearances and you let go of whatever you were using to hold yourself together and, starting at your shoulders, everything inside you just starts going soft.

"So are you and Mom getting a divorce?"

"No. Why would you think that?"

"Because you argue. You get angry at each other. And you didn't go with her to Oxford."

"Em, I didn't go with her to Oxford because we were worried about you." He grabbed my hand. "Mom and I decided that someone needed to be here for you, and since I'm not the genius with the fancy grant, I got to stay home. And there's no place I'd rather be."

Something was breaking in me. Slowly. Piece by tiny piece. Grain by grain. I tried thinking of the Arctic, of whiteness, of the frozen Earth, but nothing could stop it. Things were coming apart.

"I love your mother and she loves me and she was able to forgive me my stupidity and selfishness. Sure, we argue, but that's just who we are. We're both strong-willed and stubborn. Maybe she makes me pay from time to time for what happened in the past, but that's only fair. Marriage is a long and treacherous road, but it's also full of beauty and surprises. The one thing that's always been easy for us is loving you and your brother. That's the easy part." He looked over at me and stroked my hair. "We've been worried about you, Em, very worried. You seem troubled, like you're carrying a load too big for your fifteen-year-old shoulders. But you're also wise and thoughtful and empathetic and mature. And I guess, as hard as this is for me, you're ready for the truth."

I started to cry. Big, deep, howling sobs that came from a part of me I didn't even know was there. I let my father hold my hand. I watched the world go by. I let the truth begin to sink into me.

Mariah

I was starting to like the Greek Corner with its faux wood-paneled walls and its stained maroon carpet. I liked the sticky menus and the thick black sludge they called coffee. Silas and I were driving to Greenfield almost every day after school, and considering that graduation was right around the corner, complete with the obligatory senior-class bowling day and senior-class swim in the lake and senior-class bonfire and barbecue, I was flattered that Silas was choosing to spend his final afternoons as an Odious student in my company.

We talked. Our knees grazed each other under the table. He would take hold of my arm when he was trying to make a point and he'd leave his hand there for a few beats, and after he would take it away, I could still feel where it had been.

Much as I tried to avoid the subject, we talked a lot about Emma. His whole family was worried about her. He told me Detective Stevens wanted to come speak with her, to ask her some more questions, and he heard his father tell him no. Emma had been through enough, he said. It was time to put this all behind her.

I wondered if Detective Stevens had tried calling Mom and Carl. Did he want to talk to me? Ask me any questions? What did he want? Why was he still asking questions when this terrible episode already had an answer?

The answer was:

(a) An unshaven ghost in a red flannel jacket.

I thought, more than once, more than twice, during those beats when Silas's hand held on to my arm, when his knees were touching mine, of telling him the truth. The truth about our lie. The truth about our lie? Or was it a lie about the truth? Truth and lies. Lies and truths.

Lielielielielie. Truthtruthtruthtruthtruth.

I didn't. I couldn't. He would hate me. He would hate me for sitting across from him day after day, coffee cup after coffee cup, letting him talk about Emma and what could be bothering her when all along I knew.

Lies destroy you.

I wanted only one thing. I wanted Silas. I wanted to be alone somewhere in a room with him and have his strong arms around me and I wanted to hear him tell me that he loved me, and once I heard him say that to me, I could come clean because when you love somebody you can forgive them for the terrible things they do.

Silas said it was too nice a day to spend breathing the recycled air of the Greek Corner. Did I want to go somewhere we could sit outside?

I wanted to go anywhere he was. Anywhere we could be together. It didn't have to be alone somewhere in a room. Outside was good. Outside was open and free and there was no way of telling what might happen if we were alone outside.

We drove north. The river gets wider up north and the other side of it becomes harder to see. We sat under a tree behind a historic home where a former vice president or someone who signed the Declaration of Independence once lived. The truth is I wasn't sure who he was, except that he was someone important enough that the place where he used to eat and sleep and go to the bathroom was now somewhere you had to pay five dollars to enter.

I wondered if David Allen had gone by here on his way to Kapachuck. At night the people in dark green vests and gold nameplates who take your five dollars would have been home in their own houses with their own families, sleeping in their own beds. This house would have been empty, but it would have been locked. Alarmed against people exactly like David Allen. Maybe he came here anyway. Maybe he slept on the porch. Or maybe he slept right here, under this tree where we were sitting, with its view of the widening river.

We hadn't said a word to each other since we got out of the car. We just sat there, alone by the river, breathing the air and watching the water. I thought about how rivers play tricks on you. You think you're looking at something you've looked at countless times, but really, you're seeing something entirely new. Rivers are always moving, always changing from one second to the next. What you remember seeing the last time you stared at the river, even what you saw just before you blinked your eyes, isn't there anymore. Something new has come to replace it, and what you saw before is gone forever.

Silas was sitting with his back against the tree trunk. Some pine needles had fallen in his hair and I leaned over to brush them off. He jerked away from me and his hands flew up to his head.

I held the pine needles in my outstretched palm, to show him what I was doing touching him like that.

He smiled. "Hey," he said. "I put those there on purpose. I'm going for the outdoorsy look."

"Well, I'm sorry to say it doesn't suit you."

He picked up an acorn and threw it at me. I ducked. He threw another one.

I was laughing. "Stop it. That's so not fair. I may not look it, but I'm actually very sensitive. I bruise easily."

"Sorry," he said. "I certainly don't mean to bruise you."

He shifted away from the tree and lay flat on his back. His head was inches from my outstretched legs. He put his hands over his eyes and rubbed them.

"Oh God," he said.

"What?"

"Nothing. I'm a wreck."

I moved closer and before I knew what I was doing, or more accurately, before there was time for me to talk myself out of what I knew I was doing, I lifted his head and put it in my lap. He made a move to pull away, but I started stroking his hair, and he seemed to just surrender to this. He kept his eyes closed. I used a little bit of nail to scratch his scalp as I ran my fingers from his forehead to the back of his neck. If he'd been a cat, I'm pretty sure this would have been the moment he'd have started to purr.

"How can you be a wreck? You're Silas Calhoun."

"So?"

"So, you're Silas Calhoun. You're perfect."

"If I'm so perfect then why am I here, twenty miles away from the lake where all my friends are celebrating our high school graduation, lying with my head in the lap of my messed-up little sister's best friend?"

He opened his eyes and looked up at me, and again, before I could stop myself, I leaned forward. I let go of every thought in my head, and I tumbled into him.

Anna

When Mom came knocking on my door she was the last person in the world I felt like talking to. I wasn't sure when this happened. I used to love spending time with Mom, but these days I just wanted to get as far away from her as possible, which wasn't easy to do in our smaller-than-normal house. She always came to me with this open, pleading look like *Let's talk about something important* and sometimes I just wanted to smack that look right off her face.

I was in a bad mood. Mariah was freaking out. Detective Stevens was coming around here during his time off asking all kinds of questions that made it pretty clear he didn't believe our story. And to top it off, Tobey had canceled our plans to hang out that weekend.

sK8teR817: sorry

sK8teR817: cant be there

That's the problem with IM. You don't get a real chance to look someone in the eye and ask "Why?" What did he have to do that was more important than spending time with me? Couldn't we rearrange our plans? Find some other time to be together? Did he even like me anymore? Had he ever?

All he seemed to want to do was bombard me with questions about what happened down at the river and questions about David Allen and questions about Detective Stevens's questions. Questions all the time. But no real questions about me. Or us.

Mom knocked again. I wanted to be alone. Everyone seemed to want something from me. Tobey. Mariah. Detective Stevens. And now Mom. I couldn't just tell her to go away. I was still Anna Banana on the outside. When it came to Mom and Dad, I was still the good girl. Nice and polite. Never causing trouble.

She came in and sat at the edge of my bed. This was one of the reasons I'd always wanted siblings: to take some of the pressure off. With siblings, Mom wouldn't always be looking to have one of her "meaningful" conversations with me. If I had siblings then maybe I could mess up sometimes and still look pretty good by comparison.

My annoyance with Mom started to take shape. Why had she lied to me about my almost-siblings? Why had she told me that they didn't want more children when this wasn't true? They tried and tried and: nothing. Two miscarriages. I didn't fill them with all the love they could ever possibly imagine. They wanted more. And she'd lied about it.

"Hi, honey."

"Hi."

"Don't you think it's time to come out of your room? You've been in here most of the day. If you don't have any plans maybe we could catch a movie or something."

"Whatever happened to my Raggedy Ann and Andy dolls?" I asked.

"What?"

"I used to have them, and then one day they were gone."

"I'm sure I don't really know."

"I'm sure you do."

She narrowed her eyes and studied me. She moved closer and grabbed hold of my bare foot. "What's this really about?"

I pulled my foot away. "This is about my brother and sister. The children you hid from me."

"I'm not following you."

"When I told you I wanted a sibling you told me that you and Dad decided you didn't want any more children, that I filled you with as much love as you could imagine. And then later you told me you had two miscarriages."

"Anna, we already talked about this. You were too young then. You wouldn't have understood what a miscarriage was. I told you when you were old enough to understand."

"But it was a lie."

"Yes, it was."

"And sometimes it's okay to tell lies?"

"Yes, sometimes it is okay to tell lies."

So this was where I was going. I didn't even know it until I got there. I needed Mom to let me off the hook. Mariah wouldn't. Tobey wouldn't. Detective Stevens wouldn't. But good old Mom. She was as reliable as ever. She was always there for me. She was there when I came home from school and when I got the flu and when I needed to be let off the hook. Why was I so angry with her? I loved her. I loved her and her face with her meaningful looks.

She had reclaimed my foot and was rubbing it. It felt really nice.

"But you know, Anna, it wasn't a total lie."

"What do you mean?"

"I mean the part about you filling us with as much love as we could possibly imagine. That was and has always been the absolute truth."

I didn't say anything. I willed every part of me into the hard, round ball of my foot where her hands were applying just the right amount of pressure.

"You've done nothing but amaze us at every turn. You're smart and good and kind and intuitive. You know how to make the right decisions. You make us proud every day."

And with that, I was back, hanging on the hook.

This was an impossible situation. The walls were coming down around me, but still, I couldn't imagine telling the truth. Not now. It was too late. How could I tell Mom and Dad what we'd done? It would ruin everything. It would ruin their image of me; it would ruin every thought they'd ever had about who I was. It would be another death. Another loss. Another miscarriage.

Emma

On the Monday before graduation Silas took me out for breakfast. At this point, classes were just a formality for seniors, and Silas was attending them sporadically, which was very un-Silas-like. I had third and fourth period free. He said he thought I looked like I could use a breakfast burrito from the mall. We'd been coming to the mall for breakfast burritos since we'd moved up here. Spicy for Silas. Mild for me. They come with greasy potatoes.

I hadn't spent any time with Silas in weeks. There was so much stuff going on for seniors, all kinds of parties and events that were strictly "Seniors Only," so Silas wasn't around much lately. He said he wanted to hang out and find some time to talk. Judging from the serious look on his face, I figured it had something to do with Dad and his car-ride confession.

We were sitting in the food court in front of Benny's Burritos when I saw him. Again. This time there was no tall girl with short brown hair and knocking hips. And this time, when he saw me, he started walking toward me.

I remembered telling Anna about how that night with Owen was like a black hole. A void. A place where everything gets lost. I would have given anything, right at that moment, with Owen walking toward me, to vanish into a black hole. But the problem was this: it turns out there is no such thing as a black hole.

Time can be reversed. That's a basic tenet of quantum physics. The theory goes something like: Because the universe is infinite, nothing ever ends or disappears, and therefore information can always be retrieved and reconstructed. Through the retrieval and reconstruction of information, you can put the pieces back together and understand the past.

The black hole used to be the exception to the rule until recently, when Dr. Stephen Hawking came out against his own thirty-year-old theory about black holes, conceding that there's no such thing as a real void.

There is no place in the universe where things can disappear for good. Time can always be reversed.

"Hi," he said.

Silas looked at me with that *Who the hell is this guy?* look you would expect from a protective older brother. Especially when the guy who's coming over to talk to your sister is tall with big strong arms and sleepy green eyes.

"Hi," I said.

"Can we talk for a minute?"

I stood up quickly and almost fell flat on my face because I tried to push my chair back as I stood, forgetting it was bolted to the floor. "I'll be right back," I said to Silas, and then, "It's fine, Si. Don't worry."

I followed Owen through the food court. He was even taller than I remembered. I had to take two steps for every one of his. We weaved in and out of tables piled high with half-eaten left-behind breakfasts.

He pushed open the door to the outside and held it. A wave of hot air slammed into me. I took a seat on an empty wooden bench covered with the carved initials of young lovers who probably didn't even know each other anymore. Owen sat down next to me and now we were on more even territory. I didn't have to look up to see his face; it was right at sleepy green eye level.

He stared at me for a minute, but I wasn't going to be the first to fill the silence. I couldn't even figure out how I'd gotten here.

"Emma. I wanted to tell you that I'm sorry. I wanted to tell you that on the night of the march, but I didn't have a chance. I'm sorry about what happened to you and I can't help but feel like it's my fault."

How had I gotten here? Time can be reversed: I'd weaved in and out of the food court tables with their bolted-down chairs. I'd come to spend time with my brother with the serious look on his face. I'd taken a drive with my father, marched through the streets of my town, pulled some stuffing out of Ms. Malachy's orange couch, lost my friends. I'd gone to a party and gotten a call from my mother, *Where are you, Emma,* I'd gone to a party before that one where I had sex with Owen on an itchy floral couch.

He was sorry.

I heard the sounds of slamming doors, car engines starting and voices filled with laughter. People who'd come to enjoy another day at the mall. The sunlight was blinding me. I bent forward and put my face in my palms and tried to get some quiet and clarity in my spinning head. It started coming to me. Information slowly seeping back out of the black hole.

That night. It wasn't me. I wasn't that person. I wasn't ready to have sex with anyone. I wasn't ready to have sex with someone I didn't know. It was wrong. I didn't want it to happen. And it happened anyway.

"Emma. Are you okay?"

I kept my face in my hands and shook my head.

"I'm sorry," he said again. And then: "I should have driven you home that night. I shouldn't have let Brian drop you down by the river when it was dark. If I'd driven you home none of this would have happened. That guy wouldn't have attacked you."

"He didn't."

"What?"

"He didn't attack me."

"I don't understand."

I stood up. "I need to find my brother," I said, and I ran away.

I told Silas that I needed him to take me back to school *now*. I was crying. He asked me over and over what was wrong, who was that guy, what did he do to me. He said he'd kill him. I said just take me back to school. Please. I needed to see Ms. Malachy.

She wasn't in her office and Silas sat outside in the hallway with me, rubbing my back while I wept, waiting for her to return. He'd given up asking me what was wrong about halfway through the drive from the mall to campus.

He wanted to come in with me but Ms. Malachy said he should return to his classes. He finally gave in and walked away, with his head hanging low.

"Something is upsetting you," she said.

Even in my current state, even as I was bursting with information, newly retrieved from the depths of me, I still thought she had an annoying way of stating the obvious.

"I saw him. I saw Owen."

"And . . ."

"And I didn't want to have sex. I wasn't ready."

She took a deep breath and let it out slowly.

"Did he rape you?"

"I don't know."

How did I get here? Time can be reversed: I went to a party. I was terrible at Quarters. He was cute and he was a senior and he paid attention to me. I went along with it. I had too much to drink. I wasn't thinking clearly. I never said no.

"I don't think so," I said.

She came out from behind her desk and sat next to me on the couch. She didn't put her arms around me or touch me at all, which was what I feared she might do when I saw her coming toward me.

"What a hard time you've had this year, Emma. It's a wonder how well you've held it together. Between this and the incident by the river . . ."

"He didn't do it."

"Owen?"

"No, David Allen."

"What?"

"We made it all up. It was a lie. There was nobody down at the river that night. We were at a party."

My tears had stopped. I knew the seriousness of what I'd just revealed to Ms. Malachy, and the consequences a revelation like that might bring. But at the same time, the black hole was emptied and the endless expanse of white nothingness inside me suddenly had a horizon; it had a shape I could hold on to. Time was starting to tick forward again.

"Emma," she said. "Do you know what it is you've done?"

That was the simplest and yet the most complicated question in the universe.

We talked for the rest of the morning, sitting side by side on the couch. Retrieving and reconstructing information: Dad and his student. Owen and me. Elinor Clements. David Allen. Anna. Mariah.

When we were done, we picked up the phone and called my dad, and then we called Detective Stevens.

Mariah

Sometimes things happen. Things happen even when you don't intend them to happen. Maybe at the beginning you had good intentions, or no intentions, or intentions you thought were harmless, but before you knew it things got out of your control.

This is what I told Silas that day beside the river when he tried pushing me away, when he tried telling me that he couldn't do this.

Sometimes things take on a life of their own. You become powerless. There is nothing you can do to stop certain things from happening.

I fell into him. We rolled around in the grass and the pine needles and the acorns. Our bodies pressing into each other. I was aware of nothing but how he smelled and tasted and of how surprisingly smooth his skin was. But now he was sitting up and staring at me. He had that red-cheeked look of someone who has just awakened, slightly dazed, from a long hard nap.

"This is wrong."

I could feel his breath on my face. Warm. Like the breeze from the river.

"You're fourteen."

"I'll be fifteen next week."

"Happy birthday."

I smiled. I leaned forward. He leaned forward and pulled me onto his lap, my legs wrapped around his waist, and we started kissing again. His mouth hard on mine. Everything else fell away.

Then he pulled back again.

"Emma," he said.

Emma. The sound of her name landed with a thump. I thought in that moment about my empty life. How I had nobody. No friends to speak of. Not the kind of family you dream about. I had no one to look up to. To count on. To turn to when things got out of my control. I didn't know whose fault that was. Mine? Mom's? My absent father's? The rest of the unforgiving world's? All I knew was that right at this perfect moment, I had Silas, and I wasn't going to let him go.

I held two fistfuls of his hair. I looked into his face and noticed a small speck of gold in his left eye. "She doesn't have anything to do with this. This is just you and me. Nobody else matters."

He was perfect. Kissing him was like kissing for the first time. Nobody else had ever mattered.

"She's my sister, Mariah. This may sound strange, but I can't lie to her. Not about something like this."

On his face I saw worry and concern, but I could also see something else. I could see how much he wished we weren't down by the river, out where other people might be able to see us. I saw what might happen if we were somewhere alone with four walls around us.

I didn't want to let that look of worry and concern get between us. I felt some space opening up and I moved to close it, quickly.

More kissing. Barely stopping to breathe. His arms sleek and strong and smelling like sunblock. My hands. On his jeans. Fumbling with the buttons. He started tugging at my shirt. I thought he was trying to take it off, and I reached down to help him, I didn't care if anyone came along and saw us. But instead, he used the fabric of my shirt to pull me off his lap.

He buried his face in his knees and let out a deep, guttural groan.

"This is totally messing with my head," he said.

For a minute, looking at him sitting there, his beautiful face in his hands, I felt sorry for him. I knew what it felt like to wrestle with something. To want to do the right thing.

"I need to think about this. I don't know how to do this or if I should do this or if it's even what I really want to do. I'm sorry."

"Silas."

He lifted up his face and looked at me. I could feel that the space between us was now too big for me to bridge. I couldn't touch him. Not right then. I needed to wait. I needed him to come back to me.

"What?"

I figured I had time. I could turn my head and watch the sun on the water and sit in silence with just the knowledge that he was there beside me.

"Nothing."

If I'd known what would happen over the next few days, if I'd known that this would be the very last chance I'd have to talk to Silas, there is a world of things I might have said right then. I might have started with the truth. The truth about everything. But that isn't how time works. I didn't know then that the moment had come, that it was right there in front of me and that before I knew it, it would be gone, off down the river, never to return again.

Anna

I remember a time when nobody looked at me. When I could walk through the hallways and I was invisible. I blended in. I was ignored. Anna Banana. Anna Nobody. Plain old ordinary Anna with nothing at all to show for it.

I've said it before, but I wish I'd just told the truth. I wish I could go back and be who I was before all this happened. I miss that person. I miss that life.

When everything started to change, when I was finally noticed, it felt like the beginning of something exciting. I wasn't going to be that invisible girl forever. But what I didn't stop to think about is that when there's a beginning, there's bound to be an ending lurking somewhere right around the corner.

I just didn't know that the ending would come the way it did.

I was sitting in English class, one of the last few English classes of the year. It was Monday. School let out on Friday for the summer. Graduation was on Saturday. The afternoon was quiet and lazy. The windows were open. There was nothing to keep out: no cold, no excessive heat.

I did a kick-ass final paper on the works of Nathaniel Hawthorne. I was a good English student. I participated in class discussions. Ms. Christofar seemed to like me.

None of that matters anymore. Nothing matters other than what happened at two-fifteen.

There was a knock on the door and then it opened. Principal Glasser walked in and for a moment I thought he was just stopping by to wish everyone a happy summer and thank us for a good year but then I saw that he wasn't alone. Someone with a long shadow was standing in the hallway, just out of sight.

"I'm sorry to interrupt," Principal Glasser said. "But there is a matter of the utmost urgency."

Detective Stevens walked into the room and the door closed behind him. He was back in uniform.

Ms. Christofar sat down at her desk. Principal Glasser handed her a folded piece of paper and then he turned to face the class. "Students, I'm sure you all recognize Detective Stevens from the special assembly we held some months back."

Everyone nodded. I stopped breathing. I could feel the eyes of every person in the room.

"Well, he's taken time out from his busy schedule again

today, this time, unfortunately, not to help us as a community in our collective search for justice, but instead he's here to see that justice is done."

He looked at me. "Anna."

I stood up. He motioned for me to come to the front of the room. I neatly packed up my things. I put my backpack on my shoulders. I slid my chair under my desk and I walked forward, left foot, right foot. I didn't stumble. How I managed to function in this way I don't know, because inside, my head was filled with static. I could feel my pulse rattling my shell of a body. My face was hot. Scarlet red. Scarlet Letter. A. A is for *Anna*.

I stood at the front of the room. The stares of the students were sharp pricks in my skin, as if everyone's eyes had suddenly grown long sharp needles. But when Detective Stevens looked at me, even as his hand reached around to the back of his belt to grab hold of his handcuffs, I saw a hint of kindness in his gray eyes.

"Anna Hendricks," he said. "You have the right to remain silent."

There are certain things I never thought I'd know, like what it feels like to have those words spoken to you. I never thought I'd know that handcuffs are cold. They're heavy. They hurt.

In the hallway, Principal Glasser told me that Ms. Christofar would explain to the class why I'd been arrested. Why the same thing was going to happen to Emma and Mariah. How we had lied. We had broken the law. We had sent an innocent man to jail. We had manipulated and violated the trust of every member of this and the greater community. He said all this without ever meeting my eyes.

I'm sure I had questions, but I couldn't put them together. My mouth was parched. My throat taut as a rubber band. I would have cried, but I was all dried up. There was nothing left of me.

We rounded the corner and I saw Emma, standing next to Ms. Malachy, the school guidance counselor. Emma looked at me and I looked at her and what I wanted to do more than anything right then was the one thing in the world I couldn't do. I wanted to hug her.

Together we waited outside as Principal Glasser and Detective Stevens repeated the scene from my English class in Mariah's algebra class. My wrists shackled. My eyes cast down, locked on my black Skechers and the cold linoleum floor. I needed to stretch my neck, and when I looked up, through the small square window in the door, I saw Tobey. He was sitting in the front row of Mariah's class. I looked over at Emma but she didn't seem to notice him. Why should she? Emma didn't know anything about Tobey and me. She didn't know about our IM relationship, or about our one kiss under the dark streetlamp, at the end of a day, just before the lights came on.

He saw me too. I didn't know how to read what was on his face. It wasn't shock or surprise or hurt or disappointment. I think maybe it was something far worse. I think it was the indifferent look of someone who barely knew me at all.

My tears came, finally, in the car. I was sitting by the window. Emma was in the middle. Mariah on her other side. All three of us with our hands cuffed behind us. I realized that we hadn't been together in months. AnnaEmmaMariah. Three best friends. Three is the magic number.

Just like that night when we were alone by the river, I was the one doing the crying. But this time, nobody was talking. We weren't trying to figure a way out of the situation. We weren't plotting or strategizing or searching for a story to tell our parents. Story time was over. We all knew that this was bigger than anything we could even begin to imagine and there were no words that could be of any use to us.

When we were a few blocks from the station, Detective Stevens finally spoke.

"I'm sorry it had to be this way. I'm sorry. I'm sorry on every level."

My parents were waiting for me when we came in the back entrance. My mother wore the same blotchy look I knew must have been on my own face, brought on by all the tears.

"Oh, Anna," she said, and there was nothing she could have said to make me feel worse than the way she pronounced my name.

Since that day, the day we were arrested, the day everyone learned the truth, so much has been debated. How could we have made up that lie? Why did we make up a lie so big to cover for something so small? Didn't we know what would happen? Why did we continue to stand by our story as it grew and grew? How could three girls with our backgrounds, girls who had never been in trouble, how could girls like that do something so terrible?

But immediately after our arrest, all those good solid questions without any easy answers were overshadowed by this one other question: why did the police handcuff three young girls at school, in front of their classmates, and lead them to the back of a squad car like a group of violent criminals? Even people who hated us for what we had done thought the actions of the police were extreme. Of course there were those who thought we deserved every minute of those handcuffs and then some, but I think more people thought that what the police did to us was out of line.

They would have gone willingly, people said, and it doesn't matter that the police had more than probable cause to make the arrest. Couldn't they have brought them in without the handcuffs?

Mariah's stepfather was at the head of the pack of people who protested the arrest. He hired some famous lawyer from the city to sue the department for intentionally humiliating and degrading three minors.

I didn't hold our arrest at school or the handcuffs against the police. I know what they were trying to do. They wanted to give us some sense of the gravity of what we'd done, they wanted us to pay, and they knew we'd never serve time or even be held overnight. We'd be let go, even though David Allen spent forty-two nights at the Orsonville County Jail, and it could have been far worse. His public defender was in the process of negotiating a plea deal for him to serve seven years for assault, even though the lawyer was completely convinced of Allen's innocence. They'd decided it wasn't worth risking the trial and the life sentence a guilty verdict might bring when there were three witnesses, all prep school girls with no history of telling lies.

I'd like to believe that if it had ever gotten to that, if there had been a trial and we were called to the witness stand and sworn to tell the truth, the whole truth and nothing but the truth, that we would have done just that.

All of us.

I don't think we would have let it go any further. I can't be sure, I can't be sure of anything, but I like to believe that we never would have let it come to that.

The police were right. We went home with our parents that afternoon. We weren't held overnight. We didn't serve any time. That was never on the table. David Allen even came to our defense, asking that they go easy on us, and that maybe made me feel sorrier for what we'd done than anything else.

I was expelled from school. I got one thousand hours of community service. I began to chip away at that with a summer job at a camp for troubled children. That was kind of funny. There are many people who would have said that I should have gone to such a camp myself. Me. I used to be so perfect. Well, not perfect, but harmless, I guess.

I think it was good for me to get away from Mom and Dad for a while. We're working on getting to know each other again. I'll go to a new school in the fall. I'm going to a public school in the next county over, where you don't have to wear a uniform every day and nobody knows me. I'm kind of looking forward to that. It's never too late to reinvent yourself. I'm going to be different. No one will ever call me Anna Banana again.

Back on that day when we were arrested, while we sat in the waiting room after we'd been fingerprinted, I tried to remember what I'd talked to my parents about over breakfast that morning. It was only hours earlier, but it felt like a lifetime ago. I think maybe I complained that the milk smelled a little off. I think they both kissed me when I walked out the front door on my way to school, like they had done every morning of my life. One thing I remember for certain is that as I walked away, I looked back over my shoulder, and I waved goodbye.

Emma

Late in the summer, a pair of hikers out for the day with their black Labrador came across what was left of Elinor Clements's body, at the bottom of a ravine off the side of a mountain road, twenty miles from where she used to live. Too much time had passed for there to be a real autopsy with real answers about what exactly had happened to her, but certain things could be deduced from the circumstances. Her clothes were fifteen feet from where her skeleton lay. That told investigators that she was most likely sexually assaulted. And on her clothes was the DNA of a man with a long criminal record.

That man was not David Allen.

David Allen had been free for months and if I'd had any lingering suspicions about whether he'd been involved in her disappearance, this would have put them to rest, but I had no suspicions at all. I knew he was just another innocent victim. The world was filled with them.

I've been thinking about victimization on a spectrum. Scientists use spectrums to classify and organize information and thereby understand it better. When you know where something fits in relationship to things around it, you learn more about its nature and its parameters and what it really means.

I've met twice a week with Ms. Malachy throughout the summer. I would have wanted to meet with her anyway, but the meetings happen to be part of the deal I struck with the DA's office that kept me out of trouble. She's helping me to organize my thoughts and I've begun to understand that when it comes to sex, the spectrum from what is completely healthy and consensual to what is clearly a rape is a long and very murky line.

Some things are easy to place, like what happens between two people who respect each other and are grown-up enough to make responsible decisions. What happened to Ellie Clements occupies the extreme other end.

We've spent the better part of the summer trying to place the recent episodes of my life on this spectrum. There's what happened with Dad and his student when he used to teach in the city, and that's really hard for me to place, but Ms. Malachy keeps telling me that I should leave this episode off the spectrum altogether. It doesn't have anything to do with me, I don't know the facts, and most important, she says, I need to allow myself to just be his daughter, and to let him be my father. This wasn't easy at first, forgetting everything he told me, but just the other night I went to a movie with my parents and afterwards we went out for dinner and Dad, in his

Dad way, so completely missed the central point of the movie that Mom and I were laughing at him, hard, and the waiter had to come over and ask us to keep our voices down, and that made us all smile big broad smiles.

I don't mean to make it sound like everything is fine now. It's not. Far from it. My life is a mess. I don't go anywhere or talk to anyone. I stay home. I'm grounded pretty much forever. My parents don't let me out of their sight. Maybe it's because of the terrible lie I told, or maybe it's because they worry about what might happen to me if I go out, unsupervised, to a party where there's beer and older boys I don't know. They're also painfully aware that everyone hates me. So maybe they figure I've been through enough and they don't want me going out and having to face that.

I know they worry about me, and I'm sorry for that, but there's no going back from what happened. You can go back and understand the past, but you can't go back and change it.

I barely leave the house unless it's to see Ms. Malachy or to meet my dad for lunch at the faculty dining room. Soon I'll have to live a normal life again. Have friends. Go to school. It's hard to imagine. Silas leaves in a few days for Columbia and I've been watching him pack up his room, and the emptier it gets, the emptier I feel.

I know he forgives me. He tells me so and Silas has never given me a reason not to believe him. But on the day of our arrest, Silas went screaming into Glasser's office and then down to the police station. *It isn't true. She didn't lie. She wouldn't do that.* And then he saw me, and he knew.

Silas Devastaticus.

He forgives me now, I know. I just hope he can love me in

the same uncomplicated way he used to when I was just his little sister, before I was the girl who told the terrible lie.

The main reason Ms. Malachy and I developed the spectrum was to find a place on it for what happened with Owen. The summer is almost over and I still can't figure out where this belongs. I think it falls somewhere vaguely in the middle. It's complicated. I willingly did something I didn't want to do, even though that sounds like a contradiction. I know that I don't blame Owen. People talk sometimes about victimless crimes. I think this was like a crime with a victim, but without a victimizer.

    I've spent much of my summer writing. I wrote a letter to Owen explaining how being with him made me feel and how in the aftermath of that night I lost myself. I never sent it. I never intended to.

    I wrote a letter to Detective Stevens in which I told him that I thought he was the most principled person I'd ever come to know and how much I regretted not being able to see through the haze of my fun-house mirror of a mind and say no, this never happened. I told him that knowing he was serving our community made me feel like I'd be safe for all the days I continued to live here. That letter I sent.

    I also wrote a letter to David Allen. I don't know if he'll ever read it. I don't know if he'll ever get it. I sent it to an organization called Family of Kapachuck because they have a homeless services department, and the last I heard, Detective Stevens delivered him there, on the very same day he was freed.

    I told him I was sorry. I didn't know what else to say. There was no excuse for what I did that was worth the piece of paper I might write it on.

I don't talk to Anna much anymore. She's spending the summer as an assistant counselor at a camp for troubled children. That was part of her deal with the DA. We didn't have a big falling-out. We never screamed at each other. We never made a conscious decision to end our friendship. I don't think she was mad at me for telling the truth. I know Anna. She's a decent person, and if it hadn't been me, it would have eventually been her. It's just that after all the years of being inseparable, this incident worked itself in between us in a way that seems unfixable right now. Maybe it won't always be. Maybe we'll pass each other on the street next year, or the year after that, somewhere in between our two houses, when enough time has gone by that we can get to know each other again, as two different people.

I have no idea what happened to Mariah. I never saw her again after the day we were arrested. None of us was allowed back on campus. I had to miss Silas's graduation. My dad videotaped it, but that isn't the same. The tape is still sitting on top of the VCR. I can't even bring myself to watch it.

Principal Glasser decided to let me return this fall. I'm not really sure why. I know he didn't extend the same invitation to Anna or Mariah, who were expelled for good. It probably has something to do with being Silas's little sister or the fact that my parents are who they are at the college or maybe he has sympathy for my situation because he knows about what happened with Owen. I guess I have to get used to the fact that everybody knows everything now. That's just the way it's been since the truth came out.

Some people can't believe I'd go back, but I think it's the only way to get over this last year. I have to face who I was, and what happened to me and what I did. Running off to another school or another town or New York City would just give me a chance to start all over again, and I don't think I deserve that chance. I don't even want that chance.

I'm here. Right now. Time is ticking forward.

Mariah

School started three weeks ago and it's taken me all that time to settle in. I'm still getting used to choosing my own clothes every morning. That tacks on at least half an hour to my routine and it's a wonder I make it to classes on time. But the commute is short. My dorm is no more than a three-minute walk from the main academic building.

I didn't even put up a fight. When Carl told me the decision was final I just said, "Fine." He looked all flustered, like he'd prepared this whole speech and I wasn't even polite enough to let him have the chance to deliver it. Mom came to my room later that night. She said she was sorry but she just didn't see any other way.

"Don't worry, Mom," I said. "I don't mind. Maybe I'll even like boarding school." I smiled at her. She started to cry.

"I'll miss you."

"I know you will."

"I love you."

"Mom . . ."

"I love you, Mariah. You are my daughter, my only daughter, and you mean the world to me. But I'm doing it all wrong. I must be doing it all wrong for this to have happened. And now you're going away."

"It'll be fine, Mom. I'll be okay." I wiped a tear from her cheek. "And it isn't your fault."

What I didn't have the heart to tell her was that I agreed with Carl. I didn't fit in here. I never felt at home in his house. I never felt like I belonged. Mom seemed to be adjusting just fine to her new life, to this new family, but I felt left behind, standing somewhere by the side of a road leading nowhere. I was hoping that maybe, when I had my own room assigned in a dormitory, that that room would become mine, my own, and it wouldn't be just a room in someone else's house.

It's not so bad here. The people are kind of cool. My room has a view of the quad and right now the trees are full and there's a family of birds outside my window. The campus is pretty, and it doesn't feel like a prison even though I sleep and eat and go to all my classes here.

I knew, even in the very first minutes of arriving here, that I had to take control of how people saw me. Reputations precede you in places like this, and I didn't want to be known as that tough chick with a criminal past. So from day one, I told the truth.

Everyone always asks me why. Why would you do something

like that? Why would you make up a lie like that? Didn't you know what could happen?

All I can say is that sometimes something makes perfect sense, and then it's a complete mystery when you look at it the next day, or even the next minute, and you can't remember or explain what was so clear to you back then, because that moment is gone.

I know it sounds crazy now, but that night, making up the lie seemed like the easy way out. A harmless little lie. *You've told lies before, haven't you?* I ask them. *Everyone's told lies*. It's just that I was unable to see, right then, that the lie would gather speed and its current would carry it further and further away from me.

When I explain this, the kids here nod their heads like they understand. I'm not sure they do. I'm not sure I even do. It sounds pretty lame when I hear the words coming out of my mouth, but there's nothing else I can say about it, other than to tell the truth.

I haven't made any real friends here yet, but I'm hoping that'll happen eventually. I'm taking it slow. I like to come back to my room between classes. I keep it pretty messy. No one tells me to clean it up. It's mine. At least until next summer comes and I have to put everything I own back into cardboard boxes. But I try not to think about then.

I never talked to Silas again. It feels strange to cut off ties with someone like that without hating him. I don't hate him at all. In fact, when I come back to my room between classes and kick off my shoes and lie down on my unmade bed, I often think of him. I think of him in his dorm room at Columbia and I wonder if he likes it there. I wonder if he likes having his own place and starting everything all over. I wonder if he thinks about me. During the moments when I'm being really honest with myself, I have to admit that I doubt it. I doubt he thinks about me at all.

When I lose faith, when I think that I don't belong here, when I think that I'll just mess things up all over again, when I wonder what will become of me, I think of David Allen, and I hope that what he said is true.

After our arrest, after his release, before he walked away, he asked to speak to the chief of the police department. I'm sure they thought he was going to talk about a lawsuit or a list of demands to make a lawsuit go away, but instead he said he had only one request: don't press charges.

They're just kids, he said. *They have their whole lives ahead of them. They shouldn't be defined by this lapse in judgment. They should go on and live normal lives and not be remembered for the bad things they did. They should finish school. They should love and be loved by the people around them. They deserve forgiveness. Everyone does.*

Acknowledgments

Thank you, Douglas Stewart, for everything you do on my behalf and for always being there on the other end of a phone call or e-mail with just the right advice.

Thank you, Wendy Lamb, for taking me into the fold of Wendy Lamb Books. It is a wonderful place to be.

Thank you to everyone at Random House for all the hard work you do and have done, past and present. Thank you to Ruth Homberg, Shanta Small, Josette Kurey, Adrienne Waintraub, Alan Mendelsohn, Isabel Warren-Lynch, Stephanie Moss, Kaitlin McCafferty, Alyssa Sheinmel, Barbara Perris, Jenny Golub, Andrew Bast.

Thank you to Brendan Halpin, Andrew Sokatch, Ann Sokatch, Mary Lelewer, Justin Reinhardt, Chelsea Hadley, Stephen Reinhardt, Ramona Ripston, and Daniel Sokatch for reading this book in its various early stages and for sharing with me your invaluable comments.

Thank you to Tali Stolzenberg-Myers for teaching me about IMing and so much more.

Thank you to my D, N, & Z for everything, always.

OTHER BOOKS BY DANA REINHARDT YOU WILL ENJOY:

A Brief Chapter in My Impossible Life

★ "An outstanding first novel by an enormously talented writer." —*KLIATT*, Starred

★ "A moving first novel.... This intimate story celebrates family love and promotes tolerance of diverse beliefs. Readers will quickly become absorbed in Simone's quest to understand her heritage and herself."
—*Publishers Weekly*, Starred

★ "Superbly crafted . . . asks the big questions about love, about faith, about what it means to be a daughter."
—*School Library Journal*, Starred

How to Build a House

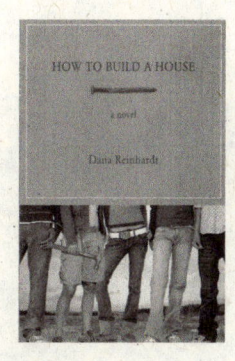

After her father divorces her beloved stepmother, tearing their family apart, Harper runs off to rural Tennessee for the summer to build a house for a family who have lost theirs in a tornado. Working alongside kids from all over the country, she meets Teddy, the son of the family for whom the house is being built. For Harper, learning to trust and love Teddy isn't easy, but it could be her first step toward finding her way back home.

NORTH HIGH SCHOOL LIBRARY
Sheboygan, WI 53083